Death Beyond the Breakers

~~ A Novel ~~

Sylvia Melvin

Sincerely,
Sylvia Melvin

This is a work of fiction. Names, character, places and events are products of the author's imagination and are used fictitiously. Any resemblance to actual persons, living or dead, locales or events is entirely coincidental.

Email: **sallymelvin6053@gmail.com**
Website: **www.sylviamelvin.com**
Blog: **http://sylviasscribbles.blogspot.com**

Also by Sylvia Melvin

<u>Mystery:</u>
Death Behind the Dunes

<u>Romance:</u>
Summer Guest

<u>Biography:</u>
Helena: Unwavering Courage
Southern Sage: The Honorable Woodrow Melvin

Acknowledgements

The thought of writing a sequel to *Death Behind the Dunes* was the farthest thing from my mind when I finished my first mystery. But, the characters have a way of 'hanging' around in an author's mind until you say, "Okay, guys and gals, let's see what crime Lieutenant Melino can solve this time."

Of course, as in the past, I had a wonderful support group. Thanks to the following individuals:

~ Captain Bill Wagner is a retired officer of the law.
~ Major Steve Collier works for Santa Rosa Sheriff's Office.
~ Cheryl and Ron Cherry are recreational scuba divers.
~ Jeff Martin is the Medical Examiner Director for Santa Rosa and Escambia Counties.
~ Sandra Enfinger and John Heflin are excellent editors.
~ Albert Melvin, my husband, is a talented cover photographer and editor.
~ Panhandle Writers Group continues to encourage and keep me focused.

Thank you.

Sylvia Melvin

Chapter One

Captain Mike Perkins looked across the emerald waters of the Gulf of Mexico to the horizon and squinted against the glare of the sinking sun. The hum of the engines of his boat, Lady of the Gulf, was a sound that still excited him after fifteen years. From the time he could cast a mullet net, fishing was in his blood. Trawling for shrimp proved to be a prosperous business. Especially, on weekends like this— Labor Day. He could almost smell that sweet aroma of grilled, fried or broiled shrimp on many a backyard or beach barbeque. It was all he could do to keep up with the public's demand.

"Hey, boss, I've got a hot date tonight," yelled one of the young hands on his crew. "How much longer we gonna stay out here? We've made us a haul today. Can't be nothin' left down there!"

A grin crept across Mike's weathered, sun bathed face but his answer was firm.

"One last pass across that shoal, Tommy. Southern Seafoods can't make a profit with empty refrigerators, not with all these folks in town celebrating the last hurrah of summer. Don't worry, your girl will wait for you. With money in your pocket and your good looks, why would she turn you down?"

"Sure, keep talkin', boss. You don't know Melanie. She could have any guy in town. All right, let's get the job done. Hey, Herbie, you handle the winch. I'll keep an eye out for snags while you lower the net."

Mike maneuvered his shrimp boat until the net was stretched out behind and it slowly sank into the gulf waters. He knew that if their luck held up, it wouldn't take long to reach their goal of loading the hold to the brim and Tommy could make his date.

A melancholy cloud drifted through Mike's thoughts as he realized there'd be no one waiting at his door. For the past year and a half he faced an empty house and a wife in prison. *Alana, how could you let greed and jealousy push you over the edge? Murdering your half-sister! Was it me who failed you somehow? I loved you so much—deep down I think I still do.*

Tears moistened Mike's eyes each time these tormented thoughts threatened to take root, but he refused to dwell on them now. Instead, he sought the one refuge that gave him peace. His forty-foot Lady of the Gulf shrimp boat transported him to a water world of ever-changing beauty and perfect solitude any time of night or day. Today was no exception.

After an hour of trawling, the crew could feel the tug and weight of the net straining the engine as the pace lessened.

"Okay, guys, pull 'er up," yelled Mike.

By now, twilight stole the light from the sun, and shadows danced across the shrimp boat's deck causing one's eyes to play tricks. As the winch drew the net out of the water and began to lower it onto the deck, Herbie let out a shout, "What's that? I can't quite make it out? Shark? Dolphin?"

"Can't be," Tommy returned. It ain't even movin'. Mike, throw the switch on the lights." Tommy started toward the suspended catch to take a closer look, then stopped in his tracks. An arm suddenly plopped over the side of the net.

The young crewman's face paled and his breathing came in short gasps. "Mike, stop the boat. Now! Get over here! Herbie keep the net steady."

Mike cut the throttle to the engines and called out, "What's the problem? We hit a snag?"

"Over there...in the net. A...a body!" Tommy's shaking hand pointed to the still form in among the shrimp.

"A body!" both Mike and Herbie called in unison.

Mike left the wheel and grabbed his twenty-year-old crew member by the shoulders. "Get a grip, son. Run back to the cabin and bring me the search lantern by the radio. Herbie, ease the net down—slowly, slowly now."

In seconds, Tommy returned with the light, and the screeching sound made by the grinding gears of the winch came to a halt. An eerie silence followed, punctuated by the waves lapping against the sides of the boat. Not one of the men uttered a word, but their eyes followed the beam from the lantern to the still form inside the net. One by one, each man moved closer as the light revealed the awful truth.

The bloated grey-skinned remains of a human being partially covered in squirming shrimp lay cold and lifeless. The fleshy part of its face, nibbled and pecked at by any number of fish and other gulf carnivores looked like ground meat.

Tommy took one glance and rushed to the side of the boat holding his stomach until his retching stopped.

Herbie looked across the net into the intense eyes of his boss.

"Captain, I'd bet my paycheck that this here's that professor who went missing a few days ago. Been all over the news. His brother claims he went fishing by himself and never came back. Still looking for his boat. You must've heard about it."

Mike's eyes never left the body as he responded. "Don't watch or listen to the TV much anymore. Had enough bad news lately what with—"

Herbie cut him off. "Sorry, boss, I get it. Didn't mean to bring up old memories. But what are we gonna do with him?"

"Leave him exactly where he is. I'll call the Coast Guard, and tell them what we've found and give them our location. My guess is they'll be over here in no time." Mike caught sight of Tommy out of the corner of his eye. "You all right?"

Tommy's response came in gulps of air. "First time I ever saw a dead body. And all chewed up like that. Man! What a sight! Yeah, I'm okay."

For the next several minutes, Mike talked to the Captain on the Coast Guard Cutter and then explained to his men, "They're about five miles away, so it won't be long. Told him we'd put up a flare. They don't want to disturb the body until the medical examiner's done his job, so I expect we'll get an escort into the bayou tonight." Mike took a deep breath before he continued, "Now let me tell you both something. This could take a while. Expect to be questioned by the authorities. Right now, we may be suspects."

Chapter Two

"Ahh, Labor Day weekend," sighed Lieutenant Nick Melino as he sank down into his recliner and reached for the TV remote. "The end of a long, hot summer and the beginning of college football. My favorite time of year."

"You talking to me, Dad, or has senility started early?" asked a young lady pulling a University of West Florida sweat shirt over her head of auburn chin-length hair.

"Just expressing some thoughts, Penny. It's been a hard-hitting week at the Sheriff's Office and I'm ready for a break. Been chasing dead-end leads on that missing prof from the university. His family reported him gone since Tuesday. You know the one—Craig Mathison, the Marine biologist that specializes in environmental studies."

"I'm taking one of his courses, Dad. He really knows his stuff. The buzz among everyone on campus is that we can't understand why he'd disappear. In fact, Jordan and I are on our way over there this evening for a student candlelight prayer vigil. What are your plans for the evening?"

"Sweetheart, need you even ask?" Nick gave his daughter a teasing smile as he pointed to the Florida Gator front and center on his blue tee-shirt.

Penny feigned a slap to her forehead. "How could I forget—opening game. Everywhere I went this week, that's all I heard. Especially on campus. Conner coming over to taunt you as usual with his Seminole chop?"

"Nope. He took Heather down to the Keys for a change of scene. My partner isn't as footloose and free as he used to be before he fell for the love of his life." Nick snickered. "Not sure I should have encouraged that relationship—might have lost a good football buddy. He told me at work last week a wedding is in the future. Wants me to be the best man."

"Yes, yes!" exclaimed Penny, dancing up and down. "They make a great couple. It's time they got serious."

"Oh, I agree, but according to Conner, Heather's been the reluctant one. It's taken her a long time to come to grips with the murder of her mother, especially since Lyndy was killed by her half-sister."

Penny's voice softened. "She'll probably never get over it. I imagine her heart's been scarred for life." She paused, her face reddening as she bit her lower lip in an attempt to stop the flow of words.

Nick saw his daughter's change of countenance and encouraged her to say what was on her mind. "And...continue, Penny."

"On a smaller scale, I can relate. Since the divorce, there are times I miss my mom, too." Tears moistened her hazel-flecked eyes and melted Nick's defenses. Instead of debating the reasons the marriage failed, he sat up and reached for Penny's right hand. She offered it freely, sniffed, and wiped at a run-away tear with her left.

"I know it hasn't been easy, honey. Your dad's a workaholic—spends too much time chasing down the bad guys and not enough with you. The sad thing is, when you work in law enforcement, your life is not your own. Your mom could never accept that."

Penny's pouting lips turned into a half-smile and she regained her composure, then bent down and gave her father a hug. "Maybe you'll find a woman who does. It's time you enjoyed some companionship with the opposite sex. That touch of grey around your temples is so darn attractive, Dad. You'll have the women beating down the door."

Nick chuckled, "Well I hope it's not tonight 'cause the only action I want to see is on the football field. Go Gators!"

Penny dropped a kiss on Nick's forehead as the doorbell rang. She grabbed her purse and called over her shoulder on her way out, "Don't wait up. Love you."

Chapter Three

"Run, run," shouted Nick into the TV screen as the Gator quarterback fought his way through a maze of opponents eager to bring him down. The roar of the crowd grew louder and almost drowned out the ringing of Nick's cell phone. *Not now. Not now.* Nick ignored the interruption, his eyes riveted to player number seven. Ten yards to go and the Gators would be on the board. Tension mounted as Nick's phone kept ringing. Suddenly, the young man's legs were no longer delivering him to a touchdown, but left the ground and flailed in the air as his opponent tackled and lifted him from behind.

"No way!" shouted Nick. Irritated, he flipped open his cell and barked into the receiver, "Melino here."

The Sheriff's Office night dispatcher recognized the edginess in Nick's tone. "It's Andy, Nick. You must be watching the game. Thought we had 'em there a minute ago. The guy runs like he's got wings on his heels."

"You're a dispatcher, Andy. What are you doing watching the game?"

"Smart phone. Not as much fun as a big flat screen, but it doesn't miss a beat."

"I know I'm on call this weekend so what's up? It better be important."

Andy's voice became serious.

"Coast Guard called a few minutes ago. They're accompanying a shrimp boat into Hide-Away Bayou. Seems the captain brought up more than a net full of shrimp."

"Oh, yeah?" Nick was all ears as his fingers lowered the volume control on the remote. "What was it?"

"A body! Some poor sucker that's been layin' on the bottom of the Gulf."

Nick let out a sigh and shook his head. "This ain't gonna be pretty—the last one gave me nightmares for a week. Andy, have you called the Sheriff yet?"

"First thing. He told me he wanted you to take the lead and meet the boat. I'll give the forensic investigator team a call now and get them on over there. Sorry to spoil your weekend but maybe the Gators will pull this one off so it won't be a complete loss."

"Hey, you're just the messenger. Get out that smart phone and cheer for me, too. Catch you later."

As much as Nick wanted to continue watching the game, duty called. He exchanged his Gator tee-shirt for a polo type with the Sheriff's Office logo displayed on the left side below the collar. As he slipped a light-weight sport jacket on, he checked the inside pocket to be sure it held his pen and notepad. He never left home without them; technology may have produced top of the line recording devices but Nick preferred his own reliable means of collecting information. It had yet to fail him. Clipping his sidearm to his belt, he headed for the door.

* * *

A sliver of moon peeked through a veil of darkness by the time Nick pulled into the Hide-Away Bayou parking lot. The moment he stepped out of his Camaro, the scent of salty water and freshly caught shrimp penetrated his nostrils. His eyes took a second to adjust to the lack of light as he searched a long pier that jutted out into a black abyss. A dozen or so shrimp boats secured in their slips gently swayed with the undulating water. Near the end of the pier, the murmur of voices caught his attention and he walked toward them.

"Evenin', fellas." A soft glow from a couple of lanterns illuminated the deck of one of the trawlers. "Looks like you're getting ready to head out. Don't you guys ever sleep?"

A hearty laugh erupted from a crew member. "Early bird gets the worm. The best catch of the day is just at sun up. Ain't nothin' like shrimpin' at night. Quiet. Peaceful."

"You lookin' for work?" asked a crewman. "We could use another hand."

"No, no," Nick replied. "I'm here on official business. Sheriff's Office." Nick suppressed a grin as immediately three smokers threw their half-smoked joints into the water. He made a mental note to mention to Narcotics that they might want to pay a call to a certain shrimp boat by the name of Sea Gal.

"Captain's inside figuring up our pay," volunteered the burliest of the trio. "You needin' to talk to him?"

The distant muffled drum beat of a diesel engine caught Nick's attention and he shook his head, "No need to bother him. I believe I hear the boat I'm waiting for off yonder ."

"Yep, just turning into the channel's my guess." A gangly, older man cocked his head and stroked an ashen beard. "Travelin' bout four or five knots, so it'll take 'bout twenty minutes before she docks. Nothin' sweeter then the sound of a diesel."

The youngest hand jumped off the boat and ran down the pier checking each slip. "Only boat not tied down belongs to Captain Mike Perkins."

Nick ears perked up at the mention of this shrimper's name. *Dear Lord, don't let it be him. The last thing he needs is to haul up a dead body.*

"Hey there, you mean the fellow who owns Southern Seafood in town?"

"Yes, sir. He's the one."

Nick took a deep sigh. This evening was turning into more than he expected. He turned and walked to the end of the pier searching the darkness for any sign of light from either the Coast Guard vessel or the Lady of the Gulf. As his eyes grew accustomed to the change, Nick saw the faint glow of the approaching vessel's lights—red on right, green on the left, with a white light centered high above the other two. This mesmerizing apparition appeared to dance on a blackened stage to the rhythm of the engine and the music made by the swaying rigging.

Headlights from a vehicle entering the parking lot bathed the whole scene with blinding light. He turned to see a van stop inches from the boardwalk. Without hesitation, the passenger side door opened and a woman in a tan jumpsuit carrying a black box jumped out and paused for a second under the pole light. Her red hair shimmered as she flipped several strands away from an oval-shaped face.

Hmmm, so this is Santa Rosa's newest forensic investigator. Conner mentioned we'd be working with a new one but he sure didn't tell me it's a female and a looker, to boot. As Nick ambled out of the shadows he observed her trim but fit physique. Not wishing to startle her, he cleared his throat and said, "Hello, there. I'm Nick Melino, Sheriff's Office." He extended a welcoming hand and was surprised to feel a rush of adrenaline as she placed her warm, soft fingers into his clasp. A deep smile that crinkled the edges of her mouth revealed perfectly formed teeth.

"So, I finally get to meet *the* Lieutenant Melino. I'm Maureen Shanesey. I have to confess your reputation has preceded you. Word around the forensic office is that you always get your man. Or woman as the case may be."

The color in Nick's cheeks deepened. "Now who do you suppose is spreading that rumor?"

Maureen's emerald eyes twinkled and she chuckled. "You might want to ask your partner. Conner's his name, correct? Had the pleasure of working with him on my first case here about a month ago. Couldn't say enough good things about his boss. But then maybe he was working on a promotion." Her laugh was musical. "At any rate, we're here to do a job, and if my eyes aren't deceiving me, that looks like a shrimp boat approaching the pier. And what's that Coast Guard vessel doing standing off at the entrance?"

Nick turned toward the Gulf. "Captain Perkins notified them he found a body in his shrimp net. Must have happened in International waters to get the Coast Guard involved. We'll take it from here, though."

Maureen nodded. "Okay, Lieutenant, let's see how strong a stomach you have. I guarantee this body isn't going to be pretty."

Nick's tone sobered as they fell in step down the pier. "I've yet to see one pulled out of the Gulf that is."

Sylvia Melvin

Chapter Four

With experienced precision, Mike Perkins maneuvered his vessel alongside the pier, through the maze of boats and up to his slip. He cut the engines back to idle so only the whishing of the water against the sides of the Lady of the Gulf broke the silence as she glided toward her mooring. Even before the shrimp boat made contact with the pier, Tommy jumped from the deck with rope in hand, ready to secure the lines.

Mike looked out the window of the wheelhouse and saw half-illuminated forms, flashlights in hand, milling about the pier. *Looks as though the law is 'Johnny on the spot', tonight. My guess, Melino's on this one.* As he stepped onto the deck, looking astern, he observed the stark white form of the Coast Guard cutter, Vigilance. It made a gentle sweeping starboard turn away from the port and faded silently away into the darkness.

More than happy to dispose of his cargo, Mike welcomed the authorities. "Hey, Melino, thought I recognized you. Hop on board. Got your work cut out for you with this one. Be forewarned. Not easy to look at."

Nick stepped from the pier onto the deck, shook the Captain's hand and replied, "Evenin', Mike. Not exactly the haul you were hoping for, I'm sure." Instantly, he turned to extend a helping hand to Maureen and continued, "Maureen, this is Captain Mike Perkins. Owns the best sea food outlet in town—Southern Seafoods." Nick turned to Mike and explained, "She's the new forensics investigator, so show us what you've got."

As Nick and the team walked toward the funnel-shaped trawl net, the muscles in his stomach tightened and he felt his body shift into defensive mode. Maureen, on the other hand, appeared relaxed and comfortable. One of her helpers produced a portable halogen light that lit up the deck as though it were daylight, sending small crabs and shrimp into a frenzy. The body lay lifeless in front of them.

"Captain," Maureen surveyed the situation, shook her head, and looked at Mike. "I hate to tell you this, but we're going to have to cut the net to remove his body. See how his limbs are bloated and his feet are tangled in the webbing."

"Do what you have to do, Ma'am. Won't be the first net I've had to mend. The timing sucks but he's gotta come outta there."

Wasting not a second, Maureen opened her black box, produced a pair of heavy-duty scissors, and handed a couple of knives to her team. Their precision cuts broke the strands of netting and freed the pale-skinned cadaver from its constraints. Like flies drawn to rotting meat, tiny crabs gnawed on slipping skin, leaving holes that revealed bone structure beneath. These tiny scavengers crawled in and out of his eye sockets seeking food from the contents of the body's most protected membrane. Decomposition was well under way, and Nick knew that facial identification would be all but impossible.

By this time, the commotion aboard the Lady of the Gulf drew attention from Sea Gal and other shrimpers who had been sleeping on their boats. Curious onlookers gathered; some even stepped aboard, rocking Mike's vessel. At this point, Nick took charge and declared the immediate area off limits. "Sorry, folks, but an investigation is taking place and we need your cooperation."

The usual mumblings rippled through the crowd, but soon everyone dispersed, and Nick gave his undivided attention back to the forensic examination.

"Thanks," said Maureen as she snapped another photo of the man's facial features. "Spectators just get in the way. I'm sure you've had to deal with your share, Nick."

"Morose, that's what it is. Don't know why human nature is attracted to the macabre. My guess is if they had to deal with death the way we do, it would soon lose its appeal. Have you found any wounds or indication of foul play?"

"Yes, head trauma. Looks as though something has grazed his scalp. I'm moving into the chest area and I see his wet suit has a couple of punctures on the left side. Could just be torn from being dragged by the boat, but let's get a closer look."

Maureen motioned to her team members. "Gavin, we need to remove this suit. I'll try to unzip while you and Sonny pull it off. Be careful, now. Ease it down."

Nick's eyes did not miss the gentleness and respect this investigator demonstrated for the dead man. Each time her gloved hands touched the dead body, Nick saw compassion in her facial expression.

An exposed bare chest provided Nick with his answer. Two small puncture wounds matched the areas of the chest where the holes in the wet suit were found. *Shot. Not drowning. Homocide, not suicide? But who was this guy?*

"Well, I believe we've located the cause of death, Lieutenant. Now it's your job to find out the who, how, and why."

The challenge in Maureen's voice ignited Nick's determination. He was not one to say 'Uncle.'

As the men on the team rolled the body onto its stomach, the larger cavity below the shoulder blade was obvious. Questions began swirling around in Nick's head as he took out his notepad and knelt closer to observe the victim's wound. "Looks to me from the size of this hole a bullet exited here. And would you not agree the tissue is beveled outward rather than inward?" Nick looked directly at Maureen.

Before she could answer, Captain Perkins cut in. "Why does that matter?"

"It tells me if he was shot in the back or if his killer blasted him from the front. And, if he was shot multiple times from the front like that, his assailant really wanted him dead and didn't want to leave a witness behind. He may have known his assailant. And, there's likely some interesting crime scene evidence out there somewhere."

"Hmm," Maureen's smile proceeded a chuckle. "Very observant, Lieutenant. Now I understand why you're the talk of the office."

Nick ignored her compliment. "Of course an autopsy will have to be done. Call me when Dr. Holmes is ready. My guess is this guy's gonna spend a few nights in the morgue especially since it's a holiday weekend."

After taking several more photos, the forensics team zipped the victim into a body bag and placed it into the van. Nick watched as Maureen directed the whole affair. She was good, thorough, and professional. He liked that. Something deep inside of him stirred, and he knew the mystery of this case was not the only thing that caught his attention.

* * *

Over the years, the initial sight of a dead body, although shocking at first, became a routine part of the job to Nick. It wasn't that he was insensitive; it was more a matter of emotional control. *Stick to the hard cold facts.* It was a mantra he repeated to himself each time he was faced with a difficult homicide. But, tonight he'd let his guard down. Perhaps it was the compassion he saw in Maureen's demeanor as she performed her duties. *It's bad enough some man's life has been taken with a gunshot. But to end up mutilated by scavengers isn't fair.* Shivers ran through Nick's body each time he visualized the tiny sea vultures feasting on decomposing flesh. Try as he might, his mind refused to erase the image.

As he approached an intersection and stopped for a red light, a flashing neon sign a block away caught his attention. Sandspur Bar and Grill beckoned Nick into a once familiar haunt. Here he could forget; here he could wash away the night's memory with an old friend—Bud.

Some country singer wailing his tale of woe enticed him into taking a table in a darkened corner. Nick surveyed the interior while waiting for the gal in the tight jeans and low-cut tee-shirt to come take his order. Not much had changed since he'd last sat with some buddies almost a year ago. Same crowd. The clink of beer bottles and glasses rang in his ears, and the smell of brew nipped at his alcoholic appetite. Guilt threatened to send him packing, but tonight's images sent another message, and he ordered not one but several Buds. He didn't simply fall off the wagon, he jumped. Settling into the comfortable chair, Nick justified his behavior as foam from the beer tickled his lips. *An AA confession will cover my tracks. How many folks have to spend their holiday weekend trying to get the image of a mutilated body out of their mind?*

Sylvia Melvin

Chapter Five

Nick was on his second cup of coffee trying to subdue a splitting headache when Penny dragged her tired pajama clad body into the kitchen. He bowed his head and buried his bloodshot eyes into the sports section. She came up behind her father, put her arms around his neck, and kissed him on the cheek. "I'm sorry, Dad. I know you're in mourning 'cause the Gators blew it last night. What happened? Guess you didn't cheer loud enough, eh?"

"Mornin' babe. Fact is I wasn't here to cheer them on at all. Missed the whole thing."

"Wait a minute. Aren't you the guy who confiscated the remote, settled into his favorite game chair, and even wore the tee-shirt with the Gator logo plastered all over the front?"

"Got a call from dispatch. I'm on duty this weekend, remember? Had to drive out to Hide-Away-Bayou. A shrimp boat hauled in a body with bullet holes in his chest, so forensics was involved. Then I had to question the captain and a couple of his crew. It was close to midnight by the time I got home."

Penny swung around to the side of the table and sat next to Nick. "I came in at eleven and thought you'd gone to bed. But come to think of it, your car wasn't in the driveway." A puzzled look crossed her freckled face and she pulled one edge of the newspaper away from Nick toward her. One look at the red spider veins on the whites of his eyes told her all she needed to know. "You stopped at the Sandspur, didn't you? Dad, you promised. And you've been so faithful attending the AA meetings." Penny's voice trembled and Nick saw disappointment in her wide-set eyes. Glistening tears pooled, then one by one spilled over onto her freckled cheeks. "I lost my grandfather to alcohol poisoning six months ago and you even admitted you could easily end up like him the way you were going."

"I'm sorry, sweetheart. His words sounded empty. "The body was..." Nick took a deep breath and stumbled. There was no way he wanted to describe what he saw to his daughter. "I took the easy way out." He closed his eyes to stop his own tears.

Touched by his emotion, Penny reached out and squeezed his arm. "I'm sure you're not the first one in the program to stumble. But Dad, please don't quit. I know you can hang in there."

A semblance of a smile on Nick's lips assured Penny he'd be back with the group come regular meeting night.

Always interested in her father's work, Penny pursued her questioning.

"So how long was this guy in the Gulf?"

"The lead investigator estimated a couple days or so. They take the water temperature as well as the amount of body decomposition to help determine the time factor. And that new forensics gal is top notch."

Penny's brows raised a little. "Oh, yeah? So you're working with her on this case?"

"Our paths are likely to pass again. I usually like to attend the autopsy. There's still a lot we don't know. Maureen will help fill in some of the facts."

Penny gave her father a teasing smile. "On a first name basis, are we? And how old is she?"

"You know, young lady, for some reason, and I can't imagine why, I neglected to ask her!" Nick winked before he continued. "I can tell you this—she's old enough to be your mother."

Penny's face brightened. "Stepmother, maybe?"

Before Nick could respond his cell phone interrupted with its usual jingle.

A quick glance at the screen told him it was business. The day was off to a busy start.

"Melino speaking."

"Nick, Sheriff Kendall here. Just got off the phone with the Coast Guard."

"Hey, they don't need to worry. We took care of the body last night. Forensics has him on ice. I'll be there for the autopsy as soon as it's scheduled."

"That's not why they called. An abandoned boat's been found tied to a piling at an unmanned oil platform about 30 miles out in the Gulf."

"So they think there's some connection to the body found last night?"

"Could be. They're calling it a crime scene. Blood's splattered on deck and shattered fiberglass is throughout the cabin."

Nick's enthusiasm heightened as he mentally ticked off what needed to be done. "Registration will tell us who owns the boat, and forensics needs to come back and take the blood samples before they get contaminated. It'd be a real stroke of luck if we got a match to the cadaver. Facial I.D. is going to be almost impossible."

"Drive over to the Coast Guard Station," commanded the Sheriff. "They'll be towing the boat into their harbor and you can take a look yourself. You've got eagle eyes, Nick. I'm counting on you."

Hmm...thank heavens you can't see them this morning, boss. His silent thought pricked a guilty conscience, and he made sure he located his sun glasses before leaving the house.

* * *

The day was sunny, the temperature a perfect 85 degrees, and the humidity nonexistent. Fall in northwest Florida was as good as it gets in Nick's opinion. Speeding along in his Camaro, with the sun roof pulled back, he let the wind clear out the cobwebs of his hangover. *Why anyone prefers the heat and the crowds of South Florida is more than I can fathom.* By the time he wheeled into the parking lot at the Coast Guard Station, Nick was back in form.

His timing was right on. Several hundred yards offshore, a smaller cutter with the empty craft in tow sliced the gentle waves as she maneuvered toward the pier, slowed and glided into her designated mooring spot.

Nick let out a low whistle as his eyes took in the 40-foot Bertram Sport Fisherman with its sleek lines, open deck and, prominent flying bridge. *Nice...very nice. Somebody put out some bucks for this one—half a mil, if it's worth a penny!*

As he waited for the okay from the Captain to board the vessel, the familiar forensics van pulled in. Two men he recognized from the previous evening climbed out and joined him.

"Mornin' Gavin, Sonny." Nick half expected to see Maureen, and a tinge of disappointment prompted him to ask, "Your boss taking the day off?"

"She usually sends us out alone if there's no body involved. Taking blood samples and fingerprints is pretty routine for us."

"Oh, yes, of course." Nick was quick to respond as a seaman walked up to them and scanned each face.

"Lieutenant Melino?"

"I'm your man." Nick reached out and shook the young sailor's hand.

"Captain says you're clear to come aboard the boat." He motioned to the other two men to follow.

Nick reached for his notepad and pen. He didn't want to miss an opportunity to get an eye witness account of this new discovery. "So I guess you were on duty when the call came in that an abandoned boat was floating around the Gulf?"

"Yes, Sir. Seems mighty strange, though. A beautiful craft like that way out yonder tied to an oil platform. 'Course Captain Gainer and Commander Lucas were the only two allowed to search for anyone. From where I stood, I saw blood all over the deck, and if you ask me, it's not from fish."

"Well, that's why we're out here," Nick assured him. "It's our job to solve that mystery."

A welcoming smile came from Captain Gainer as he stepped from the cutter. "Lieutenant Melino, good to see you again. I believe the last time our paths crossed was when that McNeil fellow was running from the law and his plane got blown out of the air over the Gulf."

Nick nodded. "Martin McNeil. The mob took care of him, but it's too bad they left a mess for you to clean up."

"All in a day's work. We were picking up pieces of floating debris for miles." Captain Gainer turned to give his attention to the latest discovery—the Maritime Explorer. "Looks as though this may be a nasty one, too, Lieutenant.

Some kind of an altercation took place on the deck, from what I can see. But that's just my opinion. You fellows are here to investigate, so climb onboard and let me know if I can be of any help. Commander Lucas was the only other person with me who walked through the boat. Sure hope we didn't contaminate any evidence. We were as careful as we could be."

"We'll get right on it," replied Nick as he stepped over the side of the vessel onto the blood splattered teak deck. Shattered shards of glass crunched beneath his feet with each step. Before he took another step, Nick retrieved his digital camera from the case that hung from his shoulder and prepared to photograph the entire exterior and interior of this crime scene. Digital photography had made his job so much easier than in the past. Now he could shoot as many photos as he wanted without fear of blowing his film budget. This way he could reconstruct the crime scene from many perspectives, lay it out on a flat surface, and examine the photos over and over. He could also manipulate the digitized images to accentuate areas of interest, sharpen and enlarge details at will. More than once, using these tools, a piece of evidence popped out at him that he or his team had not noticed at the actual site.

Stepping from the deck through a bullet-riddled sliding door into the luxurious salon with the wrap-around windows, comfortable leather couches, angled open galley, and lower control station, Nick surveyed the damage. *How many times have I seen a boat like this on the Gulf and envied the owner? What a shame! In the end, what did it get this guy? Think I'll stick to my Jon boat Dad left me.*

Nick followed a set of steps below to two spacious staterooms, where everything appeared normal and undisturbed. Confident that the crime was confined to the upper levels, Nick turned his attention to the flying bridge.

Before his foot landed on the top step, a splotch of darkened blood caught his eye.

"Hey guys! Come up here. More blood. Hmm... interesting."

Nick stepped over the specimen and looked around the functional layout. It could seat several forward and starboard and even had a small refrigerator. An extended cockpit overhang gave shade from a blazing sun. It wasn't hard to imagine someone sitting at the helm, toying with the latest large-screen electronics.

"Looks to me like the victim was shot while standing on the flying bridge and fell to the deck below," volunteered Gavin.

"I'm inclined to agree with you. There's no other sign of blood anywhere up here," answered Nick.

Sonny spoke up. "Sure is enough on the after deck. Somebody got trigger happy."

"You fellas carry on. There's got to be some bullets lodged in the salon somewhere 'cause the holes go right through the fiberglass outside wall. I'm going to take some dimensions then see what kind of projectile I can find."

Nick climbed down to the afterdeck, pulled out his notepad and measuring tape, and stepped to one side of the boat. "If you hear me muttering to myself, boys, pay no attention. I like to think out loud when I'm immersed in a scene. Drives my partner, Conner, crazy." A chuckle followed. "But that's his problem." The metal tape snapped back into its container and Nick announced, "Fourteen foot from side to side. Seven foot from stern to glass door. If he was shot from below the bridge, he fell six or seven feet." He jotted this information in his notepad then moved back into the salon.

Crawling on his hands and knees, Nick scrutinized every square inch of the teak flooring. Nothing. *Dang! I was hoping a bullet might have ricocheted and fell to the floor.* He moved to the sofa and noticed a tear in the fabric. His hopes escalated, but fell when he discovered no exit point. *It has to be imbedded in the stuffing.* With his pen knife in hand, Nick's search was halted by voices outside calling his name.

"Lieutenant Melino, I need to speak to you."

Puzzled by the request and frustrated by the timing, Nick pocketed his knife and stepped out onto the deck. Beside Captain Gainer stood a tall, thin, somber-faced man wearing a blue jacket with large yellow DEA letters emblazed across the front.

"Nick, this is Frank Salinger from the Mobile division of the DEA. I'll let him explain why he's here."

The agent offered a handshake, which Nick accepted on courtesy.

"As of this moment, Lieutenant, this boat is sealed and in custody of the DEA."

The look of surprise and shock on Nick's face brought a nervous shuffling of the Captain's feet. He braced for Nick's response.

"Under whose authority?"

"The Federal Government, Lieutenant."

Nick's eyes locked into Salinger's and the rising anger that burned in his stomach erupted in slow deliberate words. "Let me inform you, Sir, that Santa Rosa County is my jurisdiction. A crime's been committed on this boat. It's in my county and I intend to investigate until I find out who did it."

A sneer slithered across Salinger's face. "You can investigate all you want, but this vessel is off limits to you and your department."

"And why am I denied access?"

"I'm not at liberty to discuss that with anyone at your level of law enforcement."

"And why is that?" Nick shot back.

"That's just the way it is, Lieutenant. And, oh, by the way, I'm going to need those pictures you took."

"What pictures? Besides, you have a camera. You can take your own."

"Are you sure about that, Lieutenant?"

"Oh, yes. You see, that's just the way it is." Nick turned to the forensics men and called, "Pack it up guys. Looks as though we're out of here." As he walked past Salinger, Nick could not help but see the agent's arrogant expression. Another flash of anger prompted him to say, "You may have won this skirmish, Salinger but the war's not over yet."

Back at the van, a puzzled Sonny and Gavin questioned Nick. "Hey, what's going on? You ever had the DEA pull rank on you before?"

"Doesn't happen often. Usually we work together, but every once in a while a guy like him comes along. Egotistical—you know the type. I let him think he got the upper hand, but I'll get back on that boat. I have a few strings I can pull. So how did you guys do?"

* * *

Both men gave Nick thumbs up and Sonny replied, "Got samples from the deck, fiberglass walls, railings and even this." Gavin broke into a smile as his partner reached into a fold of the lab coat he had slung over his arm and produced a blood-stained gaff hook.

Nick gave Sonny a good-natured slap on the back. "Good work, man! I'll be anxious to know if the prints on that gaff match up with the guy in the morgue. Seems like too much of a coincidence that last night a body is retrieved from the Gulf, and the next day a shot-up, unmanned boat turns up."

"Well, at least the owner of the boat won't be hard to trace. A registration number will take care of that," offered Sonny. "That is, if you got it, Nick."

A smug smile preceded Nick's remarks as he opened the left side of his jacket and pointed to the inside pocket. "I wasn't just taking notes from that young sailor, fellows. This little piece of data is going to start this case rolling." Nick turned toward his car, hesitated a second, then yelled back at the two men. "Hey, tell your boss to call me if she comes up with anything new. Something tells me this is going to be one for the books."

Chapter Six

It was all Nick could do to keep from speeding as he drove back to the Sheriff's Office. A multitude of thoughts unleashed themselves as the intensity of this case began to take shape. *Who owned that boat? And what was it doing tied to an unmanned oil platform? Could the body retrieved from the Gulf be connected somehow? And why was the DEA involved?*

Nick pulled into the parking lot just in time to see Sheriff Kendall getting into a cruiser. Waving his arms to flag him down, Nick yelled, "Hang on a minute, boss. Need to talk to you."

Kendall rolled down his window and asked, "What are you doing back so soon? Thought you were checking out that boat the Coast Guard's bringing in?"

"Started to, but the DEA shut us down. What's goin' on? You know an agent Salinger? Real arrogant. Got himself some attitude."

"DEA, huh? Usually means they're on to something big and they don't want us getting in the way." Kendall stroked his chin and paused a moment. "Salinger, Salinger...yeah. I remember him. Out of Mobile. He was the lead agent in a drug smuggling case. Made the national news 'cause it involved a senator from Alabama and a nasty divorce. The wife wasn't happy with the settlement so she moved to Santa Rosa County and commenced to spill the beans. Gave us names, drop-off locations, you name it. We solved the case and Salinger's had his nose out of joint ever since. I know you won't let him intimidate you, Nick." Kimball's laugh came from his belly. "You know the old adage, 'If you can't go over the mountain, find a way around it.'"

"Gotcha, boss."

Not wishing to linger, Nick went straight to his computer and logged on to the Florida Department of Law Enforcement website and accessed the Marine Registry. His pulse quickened with anticipation as he typed in the boat's registration number. In a matter of seconds, he had his first lead. His eyes widened in surprise at the words on the screen—University of West Florida. Not sure he'd gotten the number correct, Nick flipped open his notepad again and scrutinized the numerals before him. A perfect match. *Now, why in Heaven's name would the DEA have an interest in the university?* Nick's first impulse was to pick up the phone to make a call to the university's president, but struck out since it was a holiday weekend and he was reportedly out of town. Nick sighed in frustration. He needed to make his move before Salinger stepped foot on campus.

* * *

Labor Day ushered in the official end of summer and the residents of Gulfview took full advantage of their day off. The crowded beach was ablaze with colorful fashions scattered against a white background; golfers invaded the greens, sending balls in every direction from one end of the

Dunes Gulf Course to the other; and smoke from barbeques permeated the air while families and friends gorged themselves on grilled cuisine. A festive atmosphere was in the air, but Nick could not get into it. He kept going back to the events of the past two days. For some reason he couldn't explain, his gut feeling told him there was a connection between the unknown corpse and the abandoned boat. *Tuesday morning cannot come soon enough,* Nick thought as he flipped through the phone book and underlined The University of West Florida's phone number in red.

By sunrise the next morning, Nick was awake and ready to meet the day head on. The usual traffic buildup was on the brink of becoming a problem when he turned into the Sheriff's Office parking lot. A quick survey of the vehicles indicated his partner Conner, due back today, had yet to arrive. Eager to fill him in on the case, Nick felt the adrenalin rush he always experienced when presented with a new homicide.

The smell of freshly brewed coffee lured Nick into the staff lounge. By the time he poured himself a cup and finished stirring the creamer into the black liquid, he heard Conner's familiar footsteps on the tile floor and turned to face a man in his thirties sporting an impish grin.

"Hey, boss, you're here early. What's up?"

Nick looked nonchalant and took a sip of coffee. "Oh, not much. A body showed up in a shrimp net Saturday evening, and the Coast Guard towed in an abandoned boat, shot full of holes and splattered with blood, that they found tied to an oil platform thirty miles out in the Gulf."

Conner gave Nick a questioning glance. "You serious?"

"Would I make up a story like that?" Nick shot back. After ten years of working together a comfortable camaraderie flowed between the two men. "Okay, I'm guilty of pulling your chain a time or two, but not this time."

Nick's expression turned somber, and Conner recognized the intensity in his partner's eyes. "Might have known things would liven up around here the week I go on vacation. Fill me in."

Nick motioned toward the door. "Grab your coffee and we'll talk in my office."

When both men had settled in, Conner readied himself to take notes as Nick started with the disappearance of the marine biologist from the university, described the body in the shrimp net, the boat identification, and ended with the DEA confrontation.

"Sounds as though we've got some work to do. I assume you've talked to the missing biologist's family?"

"I met with his wife and a brother. Both claimed it was not unusual for Craig to go off fishing alone."

"Any vibes about the condition of the marriage?"

"Solid family man in my opinion."

"I'll see what I can dig up about the prof." Conner's lips curled into a smile. "Doesn't hurt to have a fiancé teaching fine arts on the university staff. Heather may be some help. I'll ask her to keep an ear to the ground—never know when some obscure detail may turn up."

"Good idea. I'm going to call over there now and see if we can see the president, Dr. Tindle. I've got some questions about that boat. I hope Salinger hasn't gotten to him first. We don't need Tindle to clam up on us."

Conner was quick to respond, "Shouldn't be any problem. I needed to talk to him a month or so ago when one of their students committed suicide. Remember the kid who was diving and mixed nitrox with oxygen?"

Nick nodded and added, "You know that young man was in Penny's biology class. Shook her up because the very day he took his life she literally bumped into him. Apparently Dr. Mathison had loaned Penny a book she needed for an assignment and she was returning it. The door to his office was not quite closed and she overheard a heated conversation."

"Oh, really?" Conner urged Nick to continue.

"According to Penny, it went something like this. 'Professor Mathison, I need to pass this course. My dad is counting on me graduating Magna Cum Laude. I can't let him down. I'm begging you to give me another chance.'" Nick finished his coffee and threw his container into the trash can.

"And?"

"The prof played hardball and told him he had a history of late assignments, and the answer was no. Before she realized it, the kid bolted from the office, knocking her aside as he ran down the hallway. The next day, the news was all over the campus that there'd been a suicide. But you probably know the facts better than I since I was out of town during that investigation."

Conner nodded in agreement. "Sad situation. The boy was diving with his dad around the Oriskany. They were down below a hundred feet when the son passed out. My diving experienced has taught me that at that depth toxicity builds up in the body to the point where you are no longer conscious. Of course, his regulator dropped out of his mouth and he took in water. By the time his father realized what had happened and got him to the surface, it was too late. His family owns the Diving Deep shop down by the fishing pier. I buy all my gear there, so I'd had some contact with Kevin. Tony, his dad, was completely shattered. Hardest interview I've ever done." Conner paused a moment then went on. "I got the impression from the note Kevin left that

Tony held high expectations for his son. Maybe too high. Penny's story may support my suspicion."

"What did the note say?"

"Sorry Dad. No Magna Cum Laude. I let you down."

Nick's fingers drummed the desktop, a habit Conner came to recognize when his partner pondered a puzzling situation. A few seconds silence passed before he spoke.

"Strange isn't it that one of the professor's students is dead, the student's teacher, Mathison himself has been missing for several days, and now an expensive boat presumably owned by UWF turns up blood splattered and empty. Is there a common thread or am I stretching?"

"We won't know until we start digging, Nick." Conner looked at his watch and commented. "Make that call. Tindle should be on campus by now. Buzz me when you're ready to leave."

Conner gathered up his belongings and was halfway out the door when Nick called to him, "Hey, partner, I've got a bone to pick with you." The tease in Nick's voice was familiar.

"Oh, yeah, what's that?"

"You've been holding out on me. Didn't mention the fact the new forensics investigator you worked with on that diving suicide last month was a woman. And a mighty good lookin' one at that!"

"Aha!" laughed Conner. "So the lady caught your attention, did she? I bet it was the red hair."

"That, and the way she handled herself on the pier Saturday night. Very thorough—but still showed compassion. I admit I was impressed. So heads up, friend. When Maureen calls to tell us when they plan to do the autopsy, I'll be volunteering." Nick added with a soft chuckle, "Hey, it's a tough job, but somebody around here has to do it."

* * *

The drive onto the University of West Florida campus was a pleasant change from the constant flow of traffic heading into the city. For a quarter mile, on both sides of the roadway, a forest of arrow-straight pine trees reached toward the sky and aged live oaks spread their branches, forming a canopy for the palmetto growing beneath. The natural surroundings presented an atmosphere of serenity that was broken only by bustling students biking toward the nucleus of gray concrete buildings.

A five minute walk put the two detectives at their destination. Welcomed by Dr. Tindle, Nick sensed a warmness that indicated the DEA had not yet intervened.

"Come right in, gentlemen. Good to see you again, Sergeant Andrews, although I assume this is not a social call. We're still in shock around here with Kevin Colbert's death. A terrible waste. He had such potential. What's happening to this generation? And now we are totally baffled over the disappearance of Professor Mathison. Is that what this is all about?"

Nick spoke up first. "Sir, we're working on his case, but nothing substantial has shown up that is directly related to him yet. However, there has been a development I need some answers to. Sunday, an abandoned Bertram Sport Fisherman craft was found by the Coast Guard tied to an unmanned oil platform thirty miles off shore. When I searched the registration records, the University of West Florida came up as the owner. Is that true?"

"We do own a Bertram, Lieutenant, the Maritime Explorer. It was given to us by a philanthropist a few years ago and has been a wonderful asset to our marine biology department. Professor Mathison uses it in his research and often takes students on diving expeditions. But did I understand you to say it was abandoned?"

"Yes, Sir. And if I may speak in confidence, it may have been the scene of a homicide. There was lots of blood on the afterdeck, on the steps to the flying bridge, and on the railings."

A gasp escaped from Dr. Tindle, and the blanched expression on his face was followed by a moment of silence as he contemplated the ugly possibility. "Not Craig! Surely they wouldn't have gone that far!"

Nick and Conner exchanged puzzled glances. Often their minds worked in tandem and almost simultaneously they asked, "They? Who do you mean by they?"

"Harbor Oil Company. Ever since the oil spill, Professor Mathison has been the lead marine biologist researching and documenting the harmful effects on the Gulf. It's not good news and as you can imagine. Harbor Oil is not anxious to have these findings become public. Craig and his team recently completed a documentary to be shown on PBS next month. I'm not one to jump to conclusions, gentlemen, but do we not have probable cause for the man's disappearance?"

"Anything's possible, Dr. Tindle. You've given us information we'll use in our investigation, no doubt about that. Now, there's something else I need to tell you. For some reason, the DEA has become interested in the Bertram and they have taken custody of it. In fact, I was told the Santa Rosa Sheriff's Office no longer is in charge of the investigation."

"That makes no sense," offered Dr. Tindle. "This is your jurisdiction."

"That's the way I see it, Sir, but you may be asked by the DEA not to cooperate with us. That's why we're here now. We wanted to beat them to the punch." Conner pulled out a card and presented it to the shaken president. "We'd appreciate hearing from you if anything arises that may shed some light on the professor's disappearance."

Dr. Tindle extended his hand in acknowledging his cooperation. "More than happy to oblige. In fact, it's my duty. Craig Mathison is one of the best educators in his field that this college has ever hired. If there's anything I can do, just ask."

"Actually, there is." Nick looked at Conner, who returned a questioning glance. "I have a hunch, but I need to get fingerprints from Dr. Mathison. Any personal items that he may have in his office would suffice. Since we're here, do you mind if we take a look around? I can have our fingerprint techs on campus in an hour with a search warrant. We need to cover our bases. Wouldn't want any evidence thrown out of court."

"No problem, Lieutenant. I'll call security and they can escort you over to the marine biology department." Dr. Tindle paused and with a tease in his voice continued, "I don't suppose you're going to tell me what your hunch is all about?"

A sly smile on Nick's face erased any doubt in the president's mind. "Over the years, I've learned from experience never to show my hand until it's a done deal. And along those lines, I think it might be better if we kept this new information from the family and the media for a couple more days. No point in having them jump to conclusions so early in the investigation."

Dr. Tindle nodded as he spoke. "I see your point, Lieutenant. My lips are sealed."

"Thank you, Sir, for your time and cooperation."

Chapter Seven

With a search warrant in hand and a couple of the fingerprint techs following behind, Melino and Andrews entered the Marine Biology building. A campus security officer checked their ID and escorted them down the hall to Professor Craig Mathison's office. As the door opened, an old familiar feeling settled in Nick's gut. No matter the cause or the reason, he always felt he was invading someone's personal space. *Would I want a stranger rifling through my papers, searching every drawer in my desk, reading notes scribbled on pads?*

A quick survey of the room left no doubt a busy professor occupied this environment. A computer station with a stack of CDs haphazardly piled beside it still had its monitor light on, two five-drawer file cabinets with family photos on top stood out from a wall, a worn maroon-colored love seat sat against a beige wall, and on a black metal desk a stack of ungraded student assignments awaited. A coffee cup with an inch of cold brown sludge in the bottom sat off to the side. It caught Nick's eye immediately.

"Hey guys, lift some prints from this mug. Chances are Mathison is the only one who's touched it. Check out that picture frame, too."

Andrews put on a pair of gloves, waited for the file cabinet handles to be dusted for prints, then proceeded to open each one. "My guess is that somewhere in this room is the research material Harbor Oil does not want made public. Could be very interesting reading or viewing. I'm sure there's tons of video, too. What do you think, boss?"

"I think it's one of three places. Either PBS has it already, Harbor Oil got their hands on it, or we haven't looked hard enough. One thing I'm pretty sure of—"

"What's that, Nick?" interrupted one of the technicians.

"Craig Mathison won't be telling us. Can't wait for Maureen to give us the prints from the corpse in the morgue. I'd bet my retirement they'll match with what you fellows lift today." Nick tugged on a bottom drawer of the desk. A sigh followed another failed attempt to open it. "Might have known, locked tighter than Fort Knox. Must be something worth seein' in here. Just our luck it'd be locked."

The short tech, Gus, sauntered over to view the situation, crossed his arms, and stared at the drawer for a couple seconds. "Why don't you find your way to the men's room for a few minutes, Nick. I need to do some work here."

"You asking me to leave, Gus?"

"I think you get my drift, boss. Be back in ten minutes."

A smirk crossed Nick's face. "Conner, I think you'd better come along if you don't want to have to perjure yourself in court."

As he headed for the door, Andrews was quick to respond, "I didn't see a thing."

The two men walked to the water fountain. Conner asked, "Gus is going to pick the lock, isn't he?"

"Probably. Learned it from his cousin Vinny. The guy was a genius at it. Of course, as the Good Book tells us, our sins will find us out, and Vinny cracked one too many safes. Now, he's learning a new trade at an Alabama prison."

"So what do you think is locked up?"

"It's anybody's guess. Let's go find out."

Neither tech looked up from their work as the two detectives walked into the room. An open drawer drew their attention and Nick's face fell as he scrutinized the contents.

"Rats! All that for a stack of marine magazines?"

"Wait a minute, Nick. There had to be a good reason to lock this drawer. Those magazines may be a cover for something else. Let me in there." Conner knelt down on his knees and started to remove one magazine at a time, thumbing through each one to make sure nothing was tucked in their pages. By the time he reached for the last issue, his eyes squinted and he stared at the inside of the drawer to size up the exterior dimensions.

"Hmm, that's strange," he mused.

"What do you mean?" asked Nick.

Conner called to Gus, "You got a measuring tape in that box of tricks, Gus?"

"You bet."

Conner took the tape and measured the exterior sides of the drawer, then repeated his actions on the inside. "Eight inches on the outside and six inches deep on the inside," he said. Without hesitation, his six-foot frame was on the floor, and he inched his way on his back to look under the desk. He noticed a small hole drilled into the bottom of the drawer, so he removed a pen from his jacket pocket and stuck it through the opening. "I believe we've got us a false bottom, partner. Grab hold of the edge as I push up, will you?"

Nick immediately obliged. "False bottom. Now aren't you the clever lad! Why didn't I think of that?"

"Don't even ask, friend. Is anything budging? Let me apply a little more pressure."

The sound of metal scraping on metal was music to the men's ears as the false bottom lifted. Nick caught it between his fingers. As he lifted it out, his eyes were rewarded with the sight of a file folder and three CD jackets, each marked with the titles 'Harbor Oil Research'.

"Paydirt! Crawl out from under there, Conner, and feast your eyes on this."

Nick picked up the material and a piece of white stationary fell from the manila folder. Colored block letters, cut from a magazine, were glued to the surface and formed a sentence. A chill ran down his spine as he read the words: "Your days are numbered. You'll pay!"

By now Conner was on his feet and looked over his partner's shoulder at the blood curdling message. They both exchanged silent glances and each knew they were on the trail of Craig's killer.

* * *

Frank Salinger's chest puffed up like a peacock as he cradled his desk phone and turned to agent Cortez. "Well, well...that mystery's solved."

"Let me guess—you found the owner of the Maritime Explorer?"

"Simple matter of checking out the registration number."

"So who's is it?"

Salinger's brows knit together in a puzzled expression before he answered. "The Internet shows the University of

West Florida. Doesn't make sense. Why was it moored to an unmanned production platform?"

"And one that DEA suspects is a drop-off for drugs coming out of Honduras," replied Cortez. "According to NORAD's aerostat balloon radar records, this boat's had plenty of activity in the Gulf for the past three months and lots of visits to that platform."

Frank's expression changed. "Could be the Explorer was hijacked. From the looks of the mess of blood on the deck, there probably was a showdown, and someone got dumped. The runners use these types of boats to meet up with the drug submarines the cartels are using now."

Cortez was quick to add, "Yeah, I hate to admit it, but I guess they deserve a little credit for their ingenuity. The subs are getting more and more sophisticated and much harder to detect. And they know we haven't got the resources or the manpower to stop and search every boat in the gulf. Do you ever feel it's a losing battle, Frank?"

"We can't give up!" Salinger balled up his right fist and slammed it into his left palm. "We're too close to busting this ring. We've got us a prime piece of evidence, and the last thing I want is Detective Melino in Gulfview getting his hands on it. Besides, I smell a promotion if we shut this operation down at the oil platform." An exasperated sigh escaped from agent Salinger's lips. "Didn't expect a murder to throw a wrench into the investigation, though. We don't need the Santa Rosa Sheriff's Office snooping around asking a lot of questions. When you're trying to put a sting together, the fewer bees in the hive the better."

Cortez ignored Salinger's comment and looked pensive. "Seems strange the runner would leave a boat of that caliber behind. Maybe he ended up in the Gulf, too."

"Hope not. These guys are our only hope of getting to the kingpins. My guess is that that toadstool platform at the

East Shelf 31 lease block is the drop-off point, and either a helicopter lands and picks up the goods, or one of those high-powered crew boats from an oil company is a courier. Probably both."

"Now a yacht registered to University of West Florida suddenly appears." Cortez continues with another thought. "Don't rule out the possibility that someone with access to the boat could be trafficking on campus. College kids are a ready market."

Salinger nods in agreement and a sly smile creased his thin lips. "Good point. What do you say we head over there and take a look around. In fact, you'd make a great undercover student, my friend."

* * *

Satisfied that enough prints were lifted from the professor's office as well as the computer discs and threatening note, Nick called the search to a halt.

"We're done here for the time being, guys. Let's get these prints to the lab, and I don't need to tell you the sooner the results are available the better."

Conner spoke up. "And something tells me you and I are spending the afternoon watching a premier showing of Harbor Oil's pollution of the Gulf of Mexico. I'm a diver and it makes my blood boil to see what's happening to that environment. You'd get riled up, too, Nick if you could see what I've seen beneath the surface." Conner's voice became animated. "Hey, didn't we have a wager that if the Gators lost their first game, you'd go with me and take a diving lesson or two?"

Nick hung his head and stammered, "Well...hum."

"Sorry pal, your team let you down, and I'm going to see that you ante up on your end of the bargain. Tony down at Diving Deep is the best instructor in town. In fact, I need to get my tank refilled from this past weekend at the Keys so I'll set you up. Once you learn the basics, you'll never look at the Gulf the same again. Heather's hooked on diving. She'd stay down all day if she could."

"Okay, pal, but let me warn you. Your fiancé looks a whole lot better in a swimsuit than I do."

Conner shook his head in agreement and chuckled, "No argument there. All the more reason to keep you off the beach and near the bottom."

Chapter Eight

The aroma of cooking tomatoes, garlic, rosemary, and ground beef whetted Nick's appetite the second he opened the kitchen door.

"Please tell me you're making your Aunt Peg's spaghetti sauce, sweetie. I'm famished. No time for lunch today."

Penny scooped up a spoonful of simmering red broth and offered it to her father. "Tell me if it needs more salt. Careful, it's hot!"

Nick devoured the contents and smacked his lips. "Perfect. Peg's recipe can't be beat. You keep this cooking up and that boyfriend of yours is putty in your hands. It's not a wives' tale that the way to a man's heart is through his stomach."

Penny giggled as she stirred the pot.

"In fact," her father continued, "Next thing I know, you'll be leaving and I'll be eating cold tuna out of a can."

"Serves you right, Dad. You've been a social recluse for the past couple years. I want to hear more about that gal at the forensics department."

A dreamy look appeared in Nick's eyes and a coy smile creased the edges of his lips. "That makes two of us. I think I'm ready to step out of the shadows. Some female companionship would be a welcome change from work and a flat screen TV."

Penny gave her father a thumbs up as she asked, "So what kept you so busy you gave up lunch?"

"Actually, Conner and I were on campus today. Would you believe that abandoned boat the Coast Guard towed in Sunday belongs to the university?"

Penny's interest deepened. "Is it named the Maritime Explorer?"

"Yes. How did you know?"

"Dad, I've been on that boat. Professor Mathison uses it for diving excursions as part of his marine biology course. We get extra credit if we participate in the underwater studies. Remember, you paid for my diving lessons during the summer?"

"Ah, I do recall two or three hundred dollars my girl weaseled out of me for some extracurricular activity."

"Think of it as an investment in my future. I've really gotten a lot out of those dives. It makes everything we talk about in class come alive when you see it in front of you."

Nick removed his jacket and loosened his tie as he commented, "As a matter of fact, I may be strapping on a tank myself in the near future."

"You, Dad? What's this all about? I've never known you had an interest in scuba diving."

"I don't really, but I put my foot in my mouth as usual, and Conner's not letting me off the hook. We made a bet that if Florida lost the first game, I'd have to go diving with him."

"Dad, you can't just jump overboard with him. You'll have to take lessons."

"Oh, he's setting that all up with a guy at Diving Deep. Says he's the best instructor in the business. Tony something or other—owns the shop."

Penny's voice grew somber. "Remember the guy in my class who committed suicide on a dive a few weeks ago?" Nick nodded in agreement. "Well, Tony is his dad. Kevin was one of our group that dove for credit." A red bubble spit out of the pot and stung her stirring hand, so she turned off the burner and sat at the table.

"Really? Tell me more about that kid. Suicide is a pretty drastic step."

"Kevin hung out with a few of us during lunch, and of course we got to know him on the boat, too. He had a bit of an ego problem, always trying to impress people. Then there were other days when he just seemed to be in a world of his own. He bragged about his diving expertise and that NOAA, you know, the National Oceanic and Atmospheric Administration, were just waiting for him to graduate and he'd have a job with them. I think his father put a lot of pressure on him to be successful."

"How do you know that?"

"Professor Mathison invited Tony on one of our excursions to teach us how to go deeper and I overheard them talking about Kevin. Seems his son's grades were slipping and he wasn't pleased. It was almost like he blamed our prof."

Nick offered his opinion. "I have to admit it, honey, some parents live vicariously through their kids. Expect them to excel in areas they themselves failed in. Often it backfires and destroys relationships. Conner told me about the note Kevin left. Sounds like he couldn't handle the pressure from school and his dad, too. Tough situation."

Nick's face softened and he reached over and squeezed his daughter's arm. "All I ever expect from you is an honest effort and..." he paused a moment, "a plate of that award winning spaghetti. It's AA meeting tonight and I need some nourishment to get up nerve to confess my Sandspur sins."

Penny was quick to come back with a tease. "You might be there a while. I better dish up an extra large serving."

* * *

One of those unexpected Florida rain showers blasted pellets of water onto the highway and windshield of Nick's Camaro as he snaked his way through snail-like traffic to the Methodist church on the far end of town. A quick glance at the digital clock on the dash indicated he was going to be late. Fifteen minutes later, he drove into the parking lot and ran toward the basement door. Before entering the meeting room, he took a minute to shake the rivulets of dripping water from his jacket. As he did so, he took a quick look through the window. Seated in a circle formation were five men and two women, and one female stood with her back to him.

The moment Nick eased the door open, a voice he had carried in his head for the past several days paralyzed his movement. "My name is Maureen and I'm an alcoholic."

Shock and disbelief took his breath away, and when the group's leader welcomed him to join the others, he stammered something incomprehensible while searching for a seat. The undeniable look of surprise on Maureen's face when she realized who the latecomer was did not help the situation. By the time it was Nick's turn to introduce himself, he felt his body temperature rising and beads of perspiration running down his forehead and his graying temples.

"Sorry I'm late. A downpour held me up." *Quit stalling, man.* Nick's inner voice urged him on. *Fess up. Get it over with.* "For any newcomers," Nick looked over at Maureen, then scanned the circle, "I'm Nick. I have a drinking problem and a confession to make. Last Saturday night, I lost my self control and ended up at the Sandspur. I think you know the rest of the story. I thank God I have a daughter who loves me enough to forgive and encourage me to come back here tonight."

A man in his sixties sitting next to Nick gave him an affectionate pat on the back. "We've all been there, my friend."

As the meeting continued, Nick had difficulty giving the speaker his full attention. His eyes kept stealing periodic glances at Maureen's shimmering hair with the golden-red highlights, her porcelain skin, and eyes that looked back at him with a gentleness and a sense of understanding he'd never experienced in a woman. *What would she think of him now?*

After an hour and a half, the prayer of Serenity, spoken in unison by all present, closed the meeting. The simple truth of each line never failed to stir Nick's emotions and he recited them over again in his mind:

'God, grant me the serenity to accept the things I cannot change,

'Courage to change the things I can,

'And the wisdom to know the difference.'

Thank you, Reverend Reinhold Niebuhr. These words have gotten me through some tough times. Divorce, death, dependency on alcohol.

His moment of introspection quickly vanished when he felt a gentle nudge on his elbow. At the same time, the sweet floral scent of perfume invaded his consciousness and a coaxing voice asked, "Wanna join me in a coffee? Starbucks is just around the corner."

A smile and a deep sigh passed over Nick's lips, and his whisper was barely audible. "There is a God. Thank you."

A puzzled expression crossed Maureen's face. "Was that a yes or a no?"

"A definite affirmative. In fact, you beat me to the draw. I had every intention of asking you to join me. Let's go get a seat before this group invades the place. It's a popular spot after one of these meetings." Nick chuckled. "Starbucks knows AA members are always good for a cup of brew— coffee that is."

Chapter Nine

Seated at a corner table away from the flow of customers, Nick and Maureen settled in with their coffee. At first, an awkward silence hung in the air as if each was waiting for the other to start a conversation. Finally Maureen ventured, "Well, Lieutenant, it looks as though we share more than an interest in law enforcement. How long have you been an AA member?"

Nick took a sip of his black, scalding caffeine-laced drink before responding. His eyes tried to read the expression on her face. Was she truly interested, disappointed, or just being polite?

"One year and eight months. And you?"

"Four years next Saturday. Three of which have been total sobriety."

Nick raised his cup in a gesture of salute. "Congratulations. I've already sullied my record. Took me by surprise, too. Thought I was used to mutilated bodies, but not that latest one. Something different sent me straight to my old haunt to erase the image. Course that was just a quick fix. I paid for it the next morning."

"You referring to the guy in the shrimp net?"

Nick nodded his head in agreement as he took another swig of coffee.

"How do you do it, Maureen? You're involved on a much deeper physical level."

For a moment, sadness and unspoken pain lingered in the depths of her eyes. Her response was honest. "The support I get from the meetings keeps me away from the demons my job attracts. Didn't always used to be that way. Like you, I believed a bottle of wine every night was the answer."

"Never been much of a wine connoisseur. A six-pack of Budweiser is all I needed."

Maureen steered the conversation in another direction. "You alluded to a daughter at the meeting. High school? College age?"

"Third year in college—University of West Florida. Majoring in biology. Marine life. Penny's spent half her life in the Gulf of Mexico, so it doesn't surprise me. In fact, I'm pleased she chose that field. Maybe it'll keep her in the area." Nick gave a half chuckle, "Someone has to keep her old man in line."

Maureen's eyebrows arched in a questioning manner. "Your daughter is the only female in your life?"

Nick drained his cup dry and looked across the table at his companion. "At the moment."

"Divorced?"

"Two years. How 'bout you?"

A moment of silence passed before Maureen's voice answered with a quiver. "Five years ago my husband and three year-old daughter were in a car accident near Boston. He hit a patch of black ice, spun out of control, and hit a tree. Neither survived." Immediately, her eyes lids lowered and Nick felt a pang of guilt for asking the question.

"I'm so sorry. I should never have asked..."

Maureen cut him off. "Please don't apologize. I'm learning to live with the truth that life isn't always pretty. Sometimes it acts like a thief, stealing your very soul. I'm fighting to get it back."

"And AA is helping?"

"It's been a gift from above. AA and all that it represents is my hope."

Nick's voice took on a lighter tone. "Hey, maybe you could keep me accountable. You know, like fitness partners."

Smiling, Maureen reached across the table and extended her velvet-smooth hand. "You got yourself a deal, mister. Now tell me more about the mystery man at the morgue. Any leads yet?"

"Nothing concrete, but I've a strong hunch the shrimp boat brought up the missing professor everyone is talking about. My partner and I talked to the UWF president today and we were able to search Professor Mathison's office."

"And of course you are not at liberty to divulge what you found, right?"

Nick's face grew serious. "I can tell you this. The man had some enemies. I can't wait to see if the prints you've taken match with the ones our boys got in his office."

"The autopsy is tomorrow. Nine o'clock. I left a message on your answering machine before I left work tonight. Nick..." Maureen hesitated. "You don't have to be present. I can forward all the vital information."

Nick's voice softened. "I'll be fine. It won't be the first body I've seen opened up. It's just that if it's who I think it is, my daughter is going to take it hard. Professor Mathison is tops in her book."

Sylvia Melvin

Chapter Ten

The rhythm of Penny's flip-flop sandals on the tile floor caught Nick's attention as he sat at the kitchen table with a glass of orange juice in one hand and the morning newspaper in the other.

"What?" exclaimed his daughter. "No sizzling bacon and smell of burnt toast? Are you sick, Dad? This isn't your morning breakfast ritual."

"Autopsy today on that body the shrimp boat hauled in Saturday night. Experience has taught me it's not a good idea to go in there on a full stomach."

"Gottcha." Penny reached for a glass of her own and poured some juice.

"You're up early. Why?" questioned Nick.

"Lab work. A report's due this week." A sigh left her lips. "Sure wish Professor Mathison would come back soon. He's missed two classes now and that's not like him. He's so conscientious—always telling us how important it is to attend class on time and not fall behind."

Nick cleared his throat and his tone became serious. "Penny do you have a minute to sit? I need to talk to you."

Penny rolled her eyes and pulled out a chair. "Dad, if this is one of those parent child conversations, mom and I talked when I was thirteen."

"Okay Miss Smarty pants, I realize you're past the birds and the bees stage, but this is something I want you prepared to accept."

Penny sensed the change in her father's persona. He was now Lieutenant Melino and she gave him her rapt attention.

"If my gut feeling is correct, the fingerprints forensics are going to take today will match the prints we took from the professor's office."

The glass slipped from Penny's hand and juice ran down the edge of the table. "No, no. I can't believe that. Who'd want to kill him?"

"That's my job to find out and..." Nick placed his hand on Penny's arm and tried to soften the blow. "At this point I may be wrong. Please don't mention this to anyone. It's simply a possibility, but I wanted you to brace yourself."

Penny brushed the wetness on her cheeks away and sniffled. "You know I wouldn't compromise your investigation. I've had a similar thought since he's been a high profile figure in the oil spill scandal, but I just didn't want to admit it."

"The best thing you can do is carry on with your lab work and keep up with your studies. Life goes on."

"Speaking of such, how did AA go last night? Did you come clean?"

Nick's face flushed at the memory of the meeting, but he decided to tell Penny the facts.

"We had a new member join us. Someone I've recently met. In fact, I mentioned her to you a couple days ago."

"The new forensics examiner?" Penny's face registered disappointment. "Oh, no, Dad. You mean she's an alcoholic? I had high hopes for you that this woman might work out to be a companion. You actually showed some interest for a change."

"Whoa, young lady! Do I sense some superior attitude? That's what's wrong with society—too quick to judge. Maureen and I talked over coffee, and my opinion of her remains the same. She's a strong woman, but losing a husband and a three-year-old daughter was more than she could handle."

"Sorry, you're right. I jumped to a conclusion. I just don't want to see you hurt again. Be careful." With that, Penny kissed her father on the cheek and walked out the back door.

* * *

Still seething that Salinger denied Santa Rosa Sheriff's Office access to the Maritime Explorer, Nick planned to use the only resource readily available to him—his own photos. A call to Conner set the process in motion.

"What's up, boss?" asked his partner. "Thought you'd be in by now."

"Dr. Holmes is doing the autopsy at 9:00 a.m. on our John Doe. I told you I'd handle this one."

"With an ulterior motive," laughed Conner. "Hey, have you got your bottle of Vick's Vapor? You wouldn't want to fold in front of the lady, my man."

Nick sneered. "What do you think I am, a wimp? Just because it's routine for you young'uns to slather that stuff all over your nostrils, I don't need anything to cover up the smell. Must I remind you I've been around decaying fish all my life? Bacteria is bacteria—rotten to the core."

"Just giving you a word of caution, partner. Is that all you wanted to tell me?"

"No. Thanks to Salinger, we've got to reconstruct the interior of the Maritime Explorer. Take the photos off my camera and print them. It's in the top drawer of my desk. When I get back, we'll tack 'em up on the board and go over them with a magnifying glass. I know there has to be bullets lodged somewhere in that salon. His boys may have found them already, but we don't know for sure."

"It wouldn't be the first time photos have proved their worth," answered Conner. "See you later."

On the drive over to the morgue, Nick mentally prepared himself for the ordeal he knew would be difficult to witness. It was the one aspect of his job he found unpleasant, yet he felt it was necessary and an obligation to the victim to get to the truth. *Unlike humans, autopsies don't lie,* he reminded himself.

As he got off the elevator deep within the bowels of the hospital, Nick took a deep breath of fresh air and walked down the corridor to the specified room. Upon opening the door, a gush of gases from decomposing bodies invaded his nostrils. He stopped, steadied himself, and regained control. His eyes scanned the room like a slow-motion video camera taping the stainless steel tables, individual refrigerator units, sinks, x-ray machine, and fingerprint equipment. Hoses attached to water sources hung ready to wash blood and other body fluids into a drain. Surgical instruments, saws, knives, and scalpels lay in wait for the pathologist's skilled hand to perform his or her duty.

Nick searched the room for Maureen, but she was difficult to identify from the four other members of the forensics team. Each was dressed in medical garments from head to toe while a Plexiglas shield protected their faces. Finally, Nick recognized the tone of her voice as she directed the procedure. Although Nick knew that Dr. Holmes, the pathologist, would examine the internal organs and pronounce the cause of death, Maureen was responsible for overseeing particular aspects of the external examination.

The click of the door closing caught Maureen's attention and she walked over, smiled and handed Nick his garments.

"Good morning. I'm sure you're familiar with the visitor procedure. Slip these on. They help to protect your clothing. The gases can permeate and linger. We're waiting on the stenographer to come and take notes."

"I appreciate how sterile and clinical the room looks, Maureen. It hasn't always been this well organized."

"It's taken a few weeks to break old habits. The reputation throughout the county concerning the state of autopsy rooms hasn't always been favorable. Of course, we're a low priority on the budget, but I'm trying to change that."

Five minutes later, the stenographer arrived and the autopsy began.

One of the team opened a 40-degree refrigerator unit and rolled the body bag on a gurney out to the x-ray machine. After several views were taken from the top of the bag to the bottom, both front and back, the corpse was placed on the table. Two men removed the bag and Maureen completed the fingerprinting. After an external examination of the body, a wedding ring was removed and placed in a plastic bag.

Nick noted that each member of the forensic team went about their assigned job efficiently with a matter-of-fact attitude, devoid of apparent emotion. Picking up a scalpel, Maureen made a y-shaped incision across the chest and down the center of the body. *As usual, not much blood,* thought Nick as he became so entranced in what was taking place that the smell became a non-issue.

At this point, Dr. Holmes began to extract body organs and scrutinize them for damage. Each one was measured and then weighed in a pan attached to a hanging scale. When he looked at the victim's heart, he remarked that a bullet had severed a main artery causing death. Shattered bone fragments around the rotator cuff confirmed that another bullet had entered the shoulder and then exited the body. The doctor surmised the projectile to be one-quarter inch in diameter.

I've got to find the bullet, mused Nick.

As the examination centered on the victim's facial area, Nick felt light-headed, hung his head, and stared at the rectangular tile at his feet. He heard Maureen comment that another bullet had possibly left a grazing wound on the man's scalp; therefore, three bullets had assaulted the body.

After an hour, satisfied with the cause of death, Dr. Holmes checked his notes with the stenographer, peeled off his garments, and left the room.

Maureen walked over to Nick and placed a hand on his arm. Through the shield, Nick saw a look of concern on her face.

"You okay?"

Nick nodded in the affirmative. "The last part was hard to watch. I'll never look at a crustacean again without thinking of this poor soul. Autopsies are great motivation to get my job done."

"I have no doubt of that. I know you're anxious to get the prints so I'll get right on them. You'll have them on your desk tomorrow morning if I have to deliver them myself."

Nick's smile held a tease. "Now that's something to look forward to."

Chapter Eleven

By the time Nick got back to the office, Conner was finished printing the photos of the Maritime Explorer and was on the phone talking to a distraught female. At the sight of his partner, he switched to a conference call in order to make both sides of the conversation audible.

"Ma'am, I assure you your husband's disappearance is a top priority investigation. Lieutenant Melino is heading the team, and not one stone will be left unturned." Conner paused as she cut in with a voice teetering on the brink of unbridled emotion.

"But it's been over a week since he left the house. He's never done this in our twenty-eight years of marriage. Something's not right, Sergeant." A sob halted any further discussion, and Conner ended the conversation.

"I assure you, Mrs. Mathison, we will contact you as soon as we make some headway. Please understand that these things take time, even though I know that's not what you want to hear."

Sniffling on the other end of the line was followed by a voice struggling for composure. "I realize that. It's so hard to be patient. Thank you. I'll be waiting for your call."

Conner placed the phone in its cradle and wiped his brow. "Man, those are hard calls to take. Especially when we're withholding information about the boat."

"We'll know by tomorrow if the prints match the professor's." Nick was adamant. "I see nothing to be gained by telling them now that the Maritime Explorer was found abandoned."

Conner removed himself from the chair, stretched his arms, and asked, "So how did the autopsy go? I gather you're not in any hurry to catch lunch."

The look Nick shot Conner was more than enough to convince him that his partner was not in the mood for dark humor.

"Death by gunshot. Hit a main artery to the heart. Another bullet went through his shoulder, shattering the shoulder rotator cuff, and a third grazed his head."

"So we didn't get lucky and find some metal lodged in his body, eh?"

"Nope, so it's back to the photos. I see from the stack here that you've been busy. Bring in that portable bulletin board and let's reconstruct a Bertram salon. Apparently, that's as close as we're going to get to the real thing. My blood boils every time I think of that pompous Salinger giving me the shaft."

Conner chuckled on his way out the door. "This game's not over yet. Where's that pit bull attitude I've seen in you when the going gets tough? Look out, Salinger, my partner has you in his sights."

* * *

An hour later, Nick took another look at his notebook. *Thank goodness I had the presence of mind to sketch a rough picture of the afterdeck and the inside salon,* he thought as he arranged the photos in a useful order.

"Like a giant puzzle, isn't it, Nick? Sorta like those *Where's Waldo* books the kids love."

"I'm not sure who Waldo is, but I'm looking for bullets."

Conner handed Nick a magnifying glass. "Since I wasn't on the scene with you, explain how you think it went down."

Nick pointed to the flying bridge. "Since blood was on the steps, I think at least one bullet hit him up there, he fell to the afterdeck below, and that's where the confrontation erupted."

"So you believe he tried to protect himself?"

"Yep."

"How?"

"One of the forensics men found a bloody gaff hook."

"But he was on a fishing trip. So it could be fish blood."

"We'll know that tomorrow. Their report plus Maureen's prints should tell us a lot. Besides, there was no evidence of fish anywhere."

"Look here." Nick picked up a pencil and pointed to a photo of the glass door into the salon. He placed the magnifying glass on the spot where a bullet entered and left a hole surrounded by a spider web pattern of fractured safety glass. Nick let his pencil follow the presumed trajectory of the bullet until it rested on the breakfast bar. "Should be a bullet lodged in here. In fact..." His gaze narrowed and his pencil tapped a specific spot. "You can see the splintered wood. If Salinger's boys are on their toes, they should have seen the damage and no doubt dug around in there and retrieved it."

"Looks to me like the guy got trigger happy. Are those not two more holes in the door and one about half way up that picture window?" asked Conner.

"Follow their path and see what the bullets may have hit. They could ricochet, too, remember." Nick handed his partner the magnifying glass.

"There's a hole in the fiberglass between the door and the window...hmm. Looks as though the microwave took a hit." Conner's finger traced a dented area on its left side.

A sudden thought hit Nick and he grabbed his notebook again. He quickly scanned his writing until a sentence fragment jumped out at him. *Hole in sofa—no exit.* Once again he turned his attention to the photo of the window.

Unspoken thoughts sought answers to mounting questions. *The hole we see in the window was above the sofa. So once the bullet penetrated the glass, it couldn't change course and enter another object at a different angle. No, I see a lamp hanging over a coffee table. From the looks of things, it probably became the target for our window bullet. How did the sofa take a hit? All outside entries were accounted for.* Nick's brow furrowed as he stroked his chin and pondered the situation. *Or were they?*

"You've got that look I've seen before, boss. You're onto something, aren't you?"

"Maybe. It occurred to me that when I was in the salon searching for bullets, I was on my knees on the floor by the sofa and noticed a tear in the fabric—about cushion level. Before I could investigate further, Salinger interrupted and it was game over. Conner, I need you to go back to the computer and find this photo with the dark screens on the ventilating windows. I need a larger image than these."

"No problem. Shouldn't take but a couple minutes. Take a break. You've had a full morning."

Nick's stomach had settled back to normal after the autopsy trauma, and the thought of a cup of coffee sounded enticing. He managed to salvage half a cup and walked back to Conner's office.

"This what you're looking for?" asked Conner.

Nick looked over his partner's shoulder at the computer monitor. The texture of the black rectangular screen was smooth and unbroken until Conner scrolled down near the bottom.

"Stop! Right there. A tear in the ventilator screen. See how the threads are broken. One of the bullets went through there, and at that low level would have to hit the sofa. My guess is that the padding inside served as a buffer, and the bullet is still in there. It would be easy for the DEA to miss because, as you can see, the sofa's covering is a dark blue velour. The fibers tend to mesh together and the entry point wouldn't be obvious."

"How did you notice it?"

"Like I told you, I was on the floor running my hands under the front of the sofa and I got lucky, I guess. A shaft of sunlight illuminated the hole and it caught my attention. There it was."

"Sure," sighed Conner. "A lot of good that does us with no access to the boat."

"I don't take my orders from Salinger. Judge Ramsey and I go back a long way, and, if I can convince him that we have probable cause to search for evidence, I believe he will override the DEA. It all hangs on the fingerprints and blood samples of Mr. John Doe at the morgue. Tomorrow is shaping up to be an interesting day, partner."

Chapter Twelve

"What do you mean early release?" Frank Salinger had Brock Hamilton's attention. The biceps in Brock's muscular arms flexed as he dropped the 50-pound weight. Clanging bar bells, the constant hum of treadmills, and the chatter of the other prisoners bounced off the walls of the overcrowded weight room. An acrid odor from sweating bodies hung in the air.

Salinger's impatience and the uneasy feeling he felt mingling with felons registered in his beady eyes and chiseled face. 'C'mon, Hamilton, let's take a walk outside. I've got an offer you'd be a fool to refuse."

Brock put down the weight, picked up a towel, wiped the perspiration off his brow, and headed toward the door. Outside in the visitor's section, Hamilton, Salinger, and his partner Cortez sat in the shade beneath a sprawling live oak tree.

"Shoot," ordered Hamilton. He still maintained that toned physique he was so proud of during his time as a Marine. "Why is the DEA sending you guys to talk to me? I did all my talking three years ago and look where it landed me. I gave names of those big boys at the casino, dates, drop-off points—all the info I knew. Without my testimony you'd still be chasing their tails."

Salinger shot back. "Five years knocked off a ten year sentence is a pretty sweet deal. What I'm about to offer is the icing on the cake."

"Cut to the chase," demanded Hamilton.

Salinger wasted no time. "We know your history, Brock. Tough quarterback in high school, military stints in Afghanistan, heroin smuggling into the U.S. until you got careless and got picked up for speeding with drugs in your car. Not a smart thing to do when you're peddling illegal substances, but I guess you've learned that," commented Salinger with a smirk.

The look on Brock's face was more than enough to convince both DEA men that he was not amused. "So, what are you after? The narcs bled me dry. I have nothing more to say. It's not like I'm on the outside trafficking these days."

"You could be," offered Cortez. "On the outside, I mean."

"So that's what this is all about. You need a mole and you think I'm your man."

"Something like that," replied Salinger. "You're familiar with the Gulfview coastal area, and we need a man to work on a crew boat for the Blue Water Boat Company. We've heard rumors that this company may be involved in big time drug activity in the Gulf. Blue Water boats make all kinds of visits to any number of platforms, manned and unmanned. Lately, the Aerostat in the Big Bend and the one just west of New Orleans with those tethered, radar balloons keep tabs on things moving around in the Gulf. They've observed one crew boat deviating from the normal route several times a month and going off on its own to an area that has no oil activity. It then comes back and stops at a toadstool platform at East Shelf 31."

Cortez chimed in, "We think they're using that platform as a drop-off point since no one works there. Then smaller boats come and pick up their supply for distribution. We impounded one recently that was all shot up, and by the look of the blood on deck, the owner probably ended up in the Gulf. Possible cartel confrontation. Those boys tend to get nasty when someone invades their territory."

"It's no secret the drugs are coming out of Mexico or Honduras," added Salinger, "but we need to know how they're being transported to the crew boat, names of those involved, and schedules for pick-up and delivery. And, with your rap sheet, nobody at Blue Water would be suspicious about your presence."

Hamilton shook his head, stood up, and paced back and forth before commenting. "So far I haven't heard anything that would entice me to put my life on the line. My cover gets blown and I'm dinner for the first shark that swims by."

"How 'bout we help stage an appeal of your conviction and then drop the charges against you? Lack of evidence or some such fabrication. It wouldn't be the first time a prisoner walked free after playing ball with us."

A new look of expectation lit up Hamilton's face. "You serious? I'm outta here? What's my cover and when do I start?"

Silent satisfaction registered in Salinger's body language. The muscles in his face relaxed and he folded his arms across his chest. *Hamilton swallowed the bait.*

He went on to explain, "The owner of Blue Water Boats is innocent of what we suspect is going on. It's some of his employees working behind his back. The man's first response when I informed him of the situation was to fire them all. After he calmed down, we explained that our purpose is to shut this operation down and nail more than just a handful of crew. So things need to continue until we have sufficient evidence. Since you were a diesel mechanic in the marines, he'll hire you to work on the boat's machinery. Just happens that their main man had a heart attack, and the word is out that there's a job opening. If you agree, someone from DEA will come by tonight and pick you up. You'll be flown out to a platform, given directions on how to report to us, then board the boat in the morning."

By now the adrenaline was working its way through Brock's body, and his mind was racing at the thought of looking at the ever-changing colorful waters of the Gulf of Mexico in person, and not from behind bars. Good riddance to bars of steel. Yes, there was no doubt he'd take Salinger's offer.

A handshake sealed the deal, but before the two agents took leave, Salinger turned and had the final say. "Hamilton, one word of warning—if you double-cross us and live to tell about it, you'll be wearing stripes for the rest of your life."

* * *

Patience, Nick, patience. Nick struggled to keep hold of that thought. He held half of the fingerprint puzzle in a folder delivered to him twenty minutes ago from the lab. The ones taken in Professor Mathison's office were clear and easy to process. And thanks to the expert lab techs, the threatening note revealed Mathison's and three more unidentified prints of the probable sender.

Nick's fingers itched to get hold of those from the morgue. *As I know there's a God above, let there be a match.* His hand moved to pick up his desk phone to call forensics. Then he had second thoughts. Maureen told him she'd deliver the information first thing in the morning. A lingering sentiment could not be dismissed. *Is it the prints I'm in a rush to see, or is it her?*

Before Nick had time to come to a conclusion, Conner burst through the office door, jacket slung over his shoulder and a cell phone in his right hand. "Hey, buddy, I just got off the phone with Tony at the dive shop and we're all set up for your first lesson Saturday morning at ten o'clock. Meet me there. He teaches at his own pool, so it's private."

"But Saturday's my golfing day. You know that, Conner."

"Scratch your golf game, partner. Once you get the knack of diving, you may never want to pick up an iron again. Besides, didn't you tell me your handicap is so bad lately you're having trouble finding someone to play with?" Conner's snicker demanded a response.

"It's true. I've been a little off my mark the last couple times I played, but it happens to the best of them. Boo Weekley and Bubba Watson have their dry spells, too."

"I hate to tell you this, my friend, but their dry spells run circles around your best day, so stop trying to renege on our bet." Conner started to leave, then stopped and a boyish grin spread across his tanned face. "Hey, how would this sweeten the pot? You said Maureen is coming by the office tomorrow, right?"

Nick nodded in the affirmative. "What's she got to do with our dive lesson?"

"Invite her to join us. What better way to show her the sights than an underwater tour of the Gulf. I can assure you Heather will be there. Of course, it'll be a few lessons before open dives are on the agenda."

"Great idea!" A spark of enthusiasm danced in Nick's voice. "I bet she looks great in a bathing suit. Oops! Did I say that out loud?"

Conner let out a sigh. "Thank goodness the dating drought's over. My partner's finally crawling out of his shell. Sounding like a regular man again."

"Go home, Andrews. I've got to work on my powers of persuasion. After two years, I admit I'm a little rusty."

Chapter Thirteen

The familiar jarring buzz of Nick's alarm clock brought him to his feet and he shook his head in an attempt to clear the morning brain fog that tried to woo him back to bed for a few more minutes. His body was willing, but the anticipation of meeting Maureen plus the possible fingerprint match sent him straight to the bathroom for a shower and a shave.

Usually, he grabbed the first tie in sight, but not today. His fingers slid over the silky material of each one on the rack until he was satisfied the one he chose matched the new shirt Penny recently bought him. The scent of Old Spice followed him out the door. *Forget breakfast,* he mused. *Office coffee will do. Can't take a chance on traffic delays—not this morning.*

As he walked into his office, Nick looked around at the clutter on his desk. A stack of ongoing investigation folders threatened to fall off the edge, a napkin held half of a stale doughnut, the ever-present "Cops Are Tops" coffee mug still contained yesterday's brew, and the sports section of the local paper covered a quarter of the area. Within ten minutes he had the reports filed alphabetically in a cabinet, the doughnut stashed in the trash along with the newspaper, and he was on his way to the staff lounge to deposit the brackish liquid down the drain when Sheriff Kendall caught sight of him leaving his office. "Well, aren't we looking dapper today." Nick recognized the tease in his boss's voice and intentionally straightened his tie. "What happened to the Colombo look?"

"There's a chance I may be asking Judge Ramsey for a search warrant to get on the abandoned boat Salinger has confiscated. Want to make a good impression, you know."

Sheriff Kendall chuckled and laid a hand on Nick's shoulder. "Wouldn't have anything to do with the new forensics examiner bringing over the autopsy report would it?"

Nick's cheeks reddened. "How'd you know she was coming?"

"Andrews is in the lounge." Kimball's tone became serious. "Tells me you may be able to identify the body as Craig Mathison, the missing prof, if her prints match the ones you got from his office."

"That's what we're hoping. If that's the case, we'll make a visit to the family immediately. Mrs. Mathison has called every day."

"Let me know as soon as you get the results. Ahh..." The sheriff glanced over Nick's shoulder down the hallway. "Looks like our lady's right on time."

The click, click, click of a pair of woman's heels on the tile floor caught the attention of both men. Dressed in a navy blazer, white blouse and a gray pencil-straight skirt, Maureen carried a briefcase in one hand while a small shoulder purse hung by her side.

"Good morning," she said, exhibiting a smile that exposed pearly-white teeth.

Each man acknowledged her with a mutual greeting, then Sheriff Kendall started to move away. "Nick's been biting at the bit to see the print results, so I'll leave you two to get to work. Call me when you're finished." He turned and walked down the hallway.

Nick gave his attention to Maureen. "How about a coffee? I was on my way to the lounge to get my morning starter and I can bring one for you if you'd like."

"Sounds great. Make mine black, please."

Nick motioned toward his office. "Go ahead in and make yourself comfortable. Use my desk to display what you need to show us. I'll be right back with my partner."

By the time Conner and Nick returned, Maureen had a series of cards lined up on the desk for inspection. Each showed a fingerprint taken from the unidentified body at the morgue. After a few sips of his coffee, Nick, eager to verify his hunch that the fingerprints his lab techs took at the university would match those on his desk, pulled a folder from the file cabinet and placed several cards beneath the others.

"This is your area of expertise, Maureen. Take your time. We have to be dead on."

Conner made a nasty face at Nick and shook his head from side to side. "Poor pun, partner."

"Never the less, the truth," replied Maureen in Nick's defense. "With no face ID, fingerprints are vitally important." She picked up her high-powered magnifying glass and studied a particular card.

Nick shot Conner a smug look of satisfaction.

After several minutes of concentration, Maureen motioned for the two men to come closer. She picked a thumbprint card from both series and placed the magnifying glass over them. "Look at these loops and whorls and how they come together. They start out as separated lines but as they get closer to the tip of the thumb, they almost merge. It's the same pattern on both cards."

"So you're saying they're identical?" Nick's voice rang with optimism.

"I'd say the odds are pointing in that direction, but let me study the rest of the cards." Maureen flipped her head sideways. A few strands of her burnished hair tickled the side of Nick's cheek as he leaned over her shoulder to view the images. A tingle ran throughout his body and he knew at this moment his two-year emotional hiatus was over. *The divorce is history. I'm back in the game.* No sooner did these euphoric thoughts come to surface when his pragmatic side reminded him, *Keep your mind on your work, Nick. You've got a murder to solve.*

Conner brought his partner back to reality. "C'mon down to my office, boss. Let's leave the lady to her job. It wouldn't hurt to take another look at those photos of the boat and decide which ones will convince Judge Ramsey we need a search warrant."

"You're right. We need to get our ducks in a row. If our man is proven to be Mathison, I believe we've got a fighting chance. I'll use your computer and start typing up the request." Nick backed away from the desk. "Maureen, Conner's number is on a list by the phone. Buzz us when you've come to a conclusion and we'll be back, pronto. Okay?"

He swore he saw a twinkle in Maureen's eye and an affectionate tease in her response. "I promise you'll be the first to know, Lieutenant"

Nick closed the door and walked off with a whistle on his lips.

* * *

For the next forty-five minutes, the two detectives worked on their presentation to the judge. The tap, tap, tap of the computer keys as Nick typed up the report was the only sound that broke the silence. Conner concentrated on each photo, studying every minute detail. He placed a yellow sticky pad of paper complete with a scribbled note or two on the ones he thought best supported their request to get on the boat. As he scrutinized the last photo, a thought crossed his mind and he broke the silence.

"DEA must have reason to think that the Maritime Explorer is involved in some sort of drug activity, don't you think?"

"I'm wondering if they knew it belongs to the university, or did they find out the same way I did?" Nick replied. "Could be they suspect someone on staff is trafficking. A college campus can be a prime market."

"Good point. I can see why Salinger wouldn't want us asking too many questions, especially if they're hot on someone's trail."

Nick snorted. "That's his problem. I'm not looking for drugs. We've got a dead body and a murder to solve. I'll ask whatever needs to be asked." The ringing phone ended their conversation.

Conner took the call. "Sergeant Andrews." A momentary pause brought relief to his furrowed brow. "We're on our way, Maureen."

Before Conner could relay the message, Nick was halfway out the door. The look on Maureen's face told him they no longer had a John Doe.

"It's Mathison, isn't it?"

"I'd swear in court the prints are identical. But I've got more proof, gentlemen."

"Oh, yeah, what's that?" asked Conner.

Maureen removed slides from her briefcase and proceeded to explain. "The blood from the boat is O positive—a perfect match to the man in the morgue. Also, remember Gavin snuck the gaff hook off the Explorer. Mathison's blood type was on that, too. But here's the strange part."

"Oh, what's that?" asked Nick with increased interest.

"Another rare blood type, AB positive, trickled down the shaft of the gaff and mingled in with the O positive."

Both men looked perplexed. "Are you telling us we've got the killer's blood type?"

"I can't say it's the killer's, but someone else was on that boat. How it got there is not my area of expertise. I'll leave that to you. Of course, we're running DNA tests as well. It will take a while for that to be completed."

Nick placed one arm across his chest, bent his other elbow and rested his chin on his hand while he thought through a possible scenario.

The room went quiet except for the shuffling of feet. Finally, he looked at his companions and spoke up. "If it was the killer, Mathison may have picked up the gaff in an attempt to defend himself and struck his intruder. Those barbs can leave a nasty gash."

"Sounds plausible," confirmed Conner.

"Let me know if I can be any more help," Maureen volunteered. "I guess the next step for you is to inform the family. Oh, I almost forgot—I have the professor's wedding ring." She reopened the briefcase, extracted a plastic bag, and handed it to Nick. "His wife will be able to identify it. I don't recommend you send her down to the morgue to identify the body. We have enough proof. They need to call and tell us which funeral parlor will pick up the body and we'll have him ready."

Nick nodded and offered his thanks. "We appreciate your promptness, Maureen. You've erased a big question mark in this case."

"Hey, we're a team. Enjoyed working with you guys. See you later."

She was walking out the door when Conner caught Nick's eye and mouthed the words "diving."

Nick let her start down the hall then called, "Maureen, do you have an extra minute?"

"Sure. Did I forget something?"

"No, but I almost did. Thank goodness I have a partner who keeps one step ahead of me. Since you're new in town, I..." Nick felt his tie tighten around his reddening neck as his mind tried to untangle the words that raced through his brain. "Wondered if you'd like me to show you around the Gulf." He finally took a breath of air.

A smile he engraved in his memory took over Maureen's puzzled expression.

"Why, Nick, how sweet. I'm anxious to visit all the historical places I've read about around here."

"Well, I had something a little different in mind."

"Oh? Tell me."

"I was thinking of taking you under the Gulf. Conner says it's beautiful and once you've seen it you'll never look at our emerald water the same again."

By now, Maureen placed her briefcase on the tile floor and looked at Nick with some uncertainty. "And how are we going to get there?"

"Scuba diving. Yeah, I know it sounds bizarre, and really it was Conner's idea."

Once again her strawberry lips curled into a teasing response. "I think it's a great idea. I was on the swim team at my high school a zillion years ago, but you never forget. Don't we need to be certified? Or are you?"

"Me? Not yet. Conner is, but I start on Saturday. Would you be interested in joining us? I could pick you up."

Maureen gave Nick a pat on the arm that set his pulse racing. "Count me in. Scuba diving. Why not? See you Saturday."

With a quick adieu, Nick turned on his heel and headed back to Conner's office. *Could my day have started any better?* he mused. *I doubt it.*

In a matter of minutes, he finished the report, adding the fingerprint verdict. As the printer spit out the hardcopy, Nick felt confident he'd made a convincing argument in favor of searching the Maritime Explorer. In any event, Nick knew he held an ace up his sleeve from years past. Judge Ramsey was a man of his word and today was his chance to prove it.

Chapter Fourteen

Before any court action could be taken, Nick took a deep breath and picked up his phone. He'd made these calls to family members many times throughout his career, but it never got easier. While mentally counting down the number of rings, he loosened his tie and waited for someone to respond. At last a female voice announced, "Mathison residence."

"May I speak to Megan Mathison, please. This is Lieutenant Melino."

"Of course. I'm her sister Kathy. She's resting at the moment, but I'll go get her. For the past week, she's practically sat by the phone waiting for any word about Craig. Poor thing, she's a total wreck."

Nick cleared his throat and came straight to the point. "I think it's best you not leave her. If my partner and I could come over in the next twenty minutes I'd appreciate it."

"Lieutenant, you're not bringing good news, are you?"

"Ma'am, I'd sooner not discuss it on the phone. Just stay with her. She'll need you."

There was no doubt in the minds of the two detectives that the woman who answered the door to the

Mathison home was the professor's wife. The perky looking petite blond in the photo in Craig's office now wore a wan smile and red sunken eyes clouded with tears that threatened to spill onto her pale cheeks.

"Come in, gentlemen." She gestured to the woman beside her. "My sister, Kathy. She's been with me since Craig..." Her voice faltered and the words faded into oblivion. She fought for composure, then said, "We'll sit in the living room."

An uncomfortable silence followed everyone into the room while each settled on a place to sit. Nick sat across from Megan and simply stated, "We found your husband. I'm sorry to tell you he was a victim of homicide."

Immediately, Kathy rushed to Megan and held her sobbing sister in her arms. After several attempts to speak, in a voice gasping for breath, she asked, "How?"

"Mrs. Mathison, let me fill you in from the beginning. Saturday evening his body was brought up in a shrimp net. Forensics took him to the morgue. We had no idea who he was at that point. Then the following day, the Coast Guard towed in the abandoned Maritime Explorer, which belongs to UWF. After checking the registration number on the boat we talked to President Trindle at the university and were suspicious that the body could be that of the professor. Prints were taken from your husband's office and compared to the ones forensics examiners took at the autopsy."

"He's already had an autopsy?" asked Kathy.

Conner interjected, "Standard procedure when we have a John Doe. Besides, it confirmed he'd been shot three times."

By now both women were in tears, so Nick gave them time to calm down before he opened his leather case and extracted the fingerprint folder. "Here are the prints. Blood samples from the boat also match Craig's O positive type.

We're also running DNA tests to confirm our findings." Nick paused a moment to be sure Megan could handle his next piece of evidence. "Ma'am, what year and date were you married?"

Puzzled by the question, Megan wiped away the wetness on her cheeks before answering. "May 30, 1997. What has that to do with his murder?"

"Because you're the only one who can confirm that this wedding ring belonged to your husband." Nick handed the professor's grieving wife a gold band with their wedding date engraved on the inside.

Megan's eyes grew wider and she pressed the ring to her lips. "Bless you, bless you, Lieutenant.

"Actually, a lovely lady in the forensics department made sure you received it. She lost her husband, too, so she knew how much it would mean to you."

"You realize this case takes on a whole new perspective now," said Conner. "It's no longer a missing person investigation but a homicide. That means we need to ask questions, some may be personal, about your husband's activities."

Nick cut in. "And I'm sure once you have accepted the shock of Craig's death you'll have your own questions. Now is not the time to put you through that, so I suggest that after his burial, we spend an afternoon together. That will give us time to do some initial investigating. We know that because of the Harbor oil spill, he played a high profile part in the damage reports. Please try to recall any persons he may have mentioned involved in that affair or anything else that raises suspicion."

Megan nodded her head and with a trembling hand reached over and grasped Nick's. Her weakened voice was barely audible between gasps of breaths. "Thank you for your patience. I know I've hounded you every day since

Craig's disappearance. There is some comfort in knowing the truth."

"Just doing our job, Ma'am," replied Nick. "Oh, I want to forewarn you that the media is going to run with this story, especially the connection with Harbor Oil. My advice is to turn off the T.V. or radio. You don't need to hear about Craig's death over and over. Any new developments will be passed on to you from our office."

Kathy agreed. "Good advice, Lieutenant. I'm sure the next few days will keep us busy enough making service arrangements."

"Please let us know when that will be." As the two detectives stood to take their leave, Nick looked at Megan and said, "My daughter, Penny, was taking one of Craig's courses and thought the world of him."

This bit of comfort brought a softer expression to Megan's face. "It wasn't unusual for my husband to take a personal interest in many of his students. They felt comfortable with him. He was just that kind of guy." A new flood of wetness trickled down this grieving widow's cheeks.

"Rest assured," Conner volunteered as they walked to the front door, "we'll do everything in our power to bring justice to your family."

"Thank you," replied both women.

As the door closed behind them, Nick looked at Conner and sighed, "Now the real work begins, partner."

* * *

Fortunately for the detectives, a rescheduled court case allowed Judge Ramsey the time to hear the Sheriff's Office request for a search warrant. Nick and Conner felt the sincerity in the judge's hearty welcome as he ushered them into his office.

"Good to see you, Nick. It's been too long between visits. Hectic lives we lead, I'm afraid." His eyes shifted to Conner and Nick introduced his partner.

"Have a seat, gentlemen. I know you've heard this from me before, Nick, but it bears repeating. I am forever grateful to you for saving my daughter's life."

The look of surprise on Conner's face enticed the judge to continue his story. "When this man was a rookie cop on patrol one evening, he came upon an automobile accident. The car was in flames, and slumped over the wheel was my unconscious daughter. Without hesitating, he pulled her to safety. Today, I have grandchildren because of his actions."

"All in the line of duty, sir." A streak of red ran up the side of Nick's neck and his face flushed with humility.

"Nevertheless, I'll never forget it. Now my secretary tells me you're here on a mission. Need a search warrant, right?"

Nick handed Judge Ramsey the manila folder and explained the circumstances behind the request. After reading the report and examining the photos, the judge's expression grew solemn, his brows furrowed, and his voice grew tense. "What a shame! The loss to Professor Mathison's family, the university, the students, and to our community is profound. I will do everything I can to help you solve this case and that includes over-riding the DEA."

The sigh of relief from Nick and Conner was audible and they both extended a hand of thanks

Within minutes, with the search warrant signed, sealed, and placed in Nick's custody, the men left the court house and headed to the Coast Guard Station.

Conner looked at Nick and with a tease in his voice asked, "So you've been keeping a secret from your partner all this time? I didn't know I was riding with a hero."

"Ahh, no big deal. Any one of us would have done the same. She's just lucky I came along when I did."

"You knew Judge Ramsey would be the ace up your sleeve, didn't you?"

"He's never turned me down yet." Nick paused then continued, "They say one good deed deserves another. But I never assume anything. Some day he's going to have to turn me down."

There was little activity around the Coast Guard Station when Nick and Conner drove into the parking lot. The big boat was out and a handful of men were doing daily clean-up. After introducing themselves to the station commander, Nick presented the document that allowed access to the Maritime Explorer.

Sheltered in a boathouse, the craft sat bruised and abandoned. Once the men climbed onto the deck, each step they took crunched more of the previously shattered glass. They proceeded with caution. Nick went directly to the sofa, examined it again and located the bullet's point of entry in the couch cushion. Conner helped him turn it over in order to slash the bottom-side. Foam stuffing exploded from the seam like an over-cooked turkey. Nick's fingers massaged each piece as he sought the metal bullet fragment. Finally, he placed his hand inside the cavity and continued until he felt the evidence he sought. Confident his theory proved correct, he withdrew a one-quarter inch diameter bullet.

"Pay dirt, partner!"

"Terrific! From what I can see, the DEA boys did their job 'cause the other two bullets are not to be seen. I can see where a pen knife has scraped at a hole in the wooden bar." Conner's gaze panned the inside salon. "What I wouldn't give to own a boat like this for diving excursions."

"On our salary?! In your dreams—besides, Heather's family owns a boat building business. Something tells me once you're married, her grandmother will see to it that her granddaughter rides around the Gulf in style."

"Yeah...you think so?" Conner smiled his boyish grin. "I guess it wouldn't hurt to bring my future in-law a bouquet of flowers now and again. Just to stay on her good side."

"Hey, that gives me an idea. Remind me to call a florist when we get back."

"A florist—now I know you're keeping secrets from me. It's not Penny's birthday so it must be..."

Before Conner could finish, Nick completed the thought. "For me to know, and you to find out. Now, let's get this bullet to ballistics before they call it a day."

Chapter Fifteen

Brock Hamilton wiped sweat from his brow and sauntered into the galley of the crew boat. For the first couple days, his stomach lurched with each dip and dive in the Gulf's swells. The last thing on his mind was food, but finally his body adjusted and the smell of coffee, fried chicken and turnip greens set off hunger pangs. He still couldn't believe he wasn't locked up behind bars at night, and the thought of going back reminded him of why he was on this mission.

The fresh, pungent smell of marijuana caught his attention. He looked around the room until his eyes rested on a corner table where a tall, lean, bearded man beckoned him over.

"Bin wonderin' when you was gonna get your sea legs. Come sit down. Everybody calls me Joe."

"Thanks, think I will. I'm Brock—new diesel mechanic."

"So I've heard." Joe took a slow drag on a joint, inhaled, then offered the burning weed to Brock. "Here, help yourself. Takes the nausea away so you can fill up on some good eatin'."

As the marijuana smoke encircled Brock's nostrils, an old familiar feeling of calmness swept through his body and he relaxed against the back of the booth.

"Hear you were in the Marines and saw action over yonder. Tough guy, eh?" Joe's eyes challenged Brock's defensive nature.

"When I have to be."

"Rumor has it you were involved in more than military action in Afghanistan. Ultimately led to a little trip up the river for dealing, right?"

Brock's muscles bristled and he glared at the man across the table. "Don't see where that's any of your business. I paid my dues."

Joe's sly smile revealed uneven stained teeth and he laughed, "Whoa, man, I'm just tryin' to get to know ya. I'm wonderin' if you might be interested in a little extra cash."

Frank Salinger's undercover ploy is right on target, thought Brock as he leaned in closer and gave Joe his attention. "Sure, why not?"

Joe took a last drag on his joint, crushed the end on his dinner plate, and deposited the remainder in his pocket. "First things first. What you see on this boat stays on this boat. Understand?"

Brock nodded in the affirmative.

"We travel around from one platform to another, but two or three times a month we deviate from our route and meet some folks from Honduras who count on us to deliver goods to a toadstool platform. Do you get my drift?"

"Kinda risky isn't it with all that air surveillance of the gulf?"

"Not when we're meeting a drug sub. No radar. Totally out of sight."

"How is the exchange made?"

"A diver. Had us a college kid this past summer who came out on weekends, but he up and quit on us a month or so ago. Had himself a good business on campus but..." Joe paused and thought a moment. "DEA must have nailed him, cause he disappeared and we ain't seen hide nor hair of him."

"So where do I come in? I don't dive, so I'm no help there."

"Extra pair of eyes. Never know when a drug enforcement agent is in an undercover boat." A sinister laugh sent chills down Brock's spine. "But we got ways to deal with them—there's a lot of water in the gulf. Most of them are never found."

"So tell me again what happens at the toadstool."

"Since it's an unmanned platform, fairly isolated, there's not too much activity around. A perfect spot to transfer the goods. Fifty feet down the shaft a container is attached to one of the legs—covered in barnacles and not very obvious. The drugs are in water-proof boxes so our diver simply deposits them."

"Who picks them up?" Brock hoped Joe would reveal the information Salinger counted on him to get, but no such luck. *He doesn't trust me yet,* thought Brock. *He's already told me more than he should have.*

Joe stroked his chin and his cold blue eyes remained fixed on Brock. "I've heard the casinos may be involved. Be prepared to take a side trip this week. We have a replacement diver in Morgan City who can't wait to get in on the action." Joe got up from the table and held out his hand. "Welcome aboard. Hey, you better get you some of that chicken before the cook throws it overboard to the sharks."

Brock shook his mate's hand. "I believe I will. You'll find me in the engine room if we need to talk some more." He smiled to himself as he picked up a plate and utensils. *This mole business just might work out all right.*

Sylvia Melvin

Chapter Sixteen

Butterflies danced in Nick's stomach the moment he awoke. He glanced at the bedside clock through sleep-laden eyes and tried to remember why he set the alarm to waken him this early on a Saturday morning. His muddled thoughts finally connected to the odd feeling that surged through his body .

Oh yeah, this is the day I put my life in the hands of some scuba diving instructor. I'll never bet with Conner again. Maybe it's not too late to cancel. Tell him I've come down with a serious intestinal disorder.

As sanity slowly returned through his grogginess, Nick remembered Maureen agreed to accompany him. The thought of spending a few hours with her quickened his actions and within thirty minutes he'd showered, shaved, and dressed in navy shorts and his beloved Gator tee-shirt. Not sure if he'd need them yet, he tossed a backpack containing a swim suit, towel, and a couple bottles of water onto the back seat of his Camaro and sped off toward Bayfront Condos.

Nick felt like a nervous teenager on his first date as he walked up the steps and reached for the door bell. His finger barely touched it when the door opened, and he felt soft, warm lips graze his cheek. The sweet smell of lavender lingered as Maureen withdrew and invited him in.

"Wow! Let me ring the bell again," he teased. "It's too early in the day for me to have done anything to deserve that."

A pink blush complimented the peasant-style blouse and white Capris she wore that revealed smooth sun-tanned legs.

"Thank you for the flowers. What a sweet gesture on your part. You remembered our conversation. No one's ever helped me celebrate my sobriety anniversary."

"Maybe that's because only we kindred folk understand how important it is." For a second their eyes locked and Maureen saw the depth of Nick's sincerity.

"I'll get my things," she stammered and flung a French braid over her shoulder.

Conner and Heather stood waiting at the entrance to Diving Deep as Maureen and Nick drove into a parking space.

"Hey, who's the blonde with your partner? She's very attractive."

"The daughter of a woman I used to know. Remind me and I'll tell you her story over dinner some evening." Nick looked with baited breath for a spark of interest.

Maureen gave him a sideways glance and smiled. "I'd like that."

Conner yelled across the parking lot as he looked at his watch, "C'mon, partner! Time's a wastin'."

Nick introduced the women and the four of them entered Diving Deep, a small but well-stocked shop. Goggles, fins, gloves, snorkel and diving gear covered every inch of wall space and the smell of neoprene, a material in the wet suits, filled the air. A display of swim suits, cover-ups, and hats caught the ladies' eyes and before long the women were in deep discussion over the best sunscreen to wear.

After a few minutes, a tall, tanned, and muscular male with a closely shaven head entered the room and walked over to Conner.

"Hi, folks. Sorry for the wait. Red Cross callin' for my blood again. He nodded at Conner then turned to Nick and extended his hand. "I'm Tony."

Nick responded with a handshake. "Nick Melino, and my friend is Maureen Shenesey."

"My pleasure, ma'am."

The look of approval on Tony's face gave Nick an uneasy feeling. *I don't need any competition*, Nick mused.

Conner interrupted the introductions and turned to Nick. "You guys don't need us now, so Heather and I are off to find a place on the beach for our wedding reception. If it was up to me, we'd just light up some grills and throw on a few pounds of shrimp, but these women have other ideas."

Heather gave her fiancé a playful jab in the ribs. "Conner, now you know my grandmother has been waiting to pull out all the stops for our wedding. What she couldn't do for mom, she wants to do for us. And barbecued shrimp is just not going to cut it."

"Well, if it would make her happy, we could grill filet mignon along with it. Sort of a surf and turf."

Heather feigned a look of exasperation, grabbed hold of Conner's arm, and ushered him toward the door.

"Adorable couple," said Maureen. "I take it the grandmother is well off financially."

"Owns Seaworthy Boats," explained Nick. "Been in business here since the Thirties. Quality sells, and they're one of the best."

"Speaking of fancy boats," Tony entered the conversation, "today's paper claims that The University of

West Florida owns that Bertram the Coast Guard found abandoned. Is that a fact?"

Nick nodded his head in the affirmative.

"According to the story," continued Tony, "the Sheriff's Office positively identified a body pulled out of the Gulf as Professor Mathison. The university is saying he was the last person to use the boat. In my opinion, a man shouldn't be out there these days alone. Not with all the pirating going on. Of course, I understand the prof was on Harbor Oil's tail over the spill, too. Should have known better than to play hardball with a big league oil company. Wouldn't be the first time they covered something up. But I guess this is old news to you folks. You work fast, Lieutenant."

"We do our best."

"Well, you're not here to talk shop, so let's go to the back room where we'll start the first class. Oh, did Conner tell you the money's due up front?" Tony smirked and gave a slight chuckle. "Tends to keep folks committed to the course."

The moment Nick and Maureen entered the makeshift classroom they felt the presence of another person. Photos of a young man at various stages of his life covered the walls. There were pictures of him receiving educational awards, swimming medals, and scuba diving. The most prominent one—of father and son—brought a tear to Maureen's eye. A glass case displayed several athletic trophies and blue ribbons.

Compelled to comment on this shrine-like display, Nick expressed his feelings. "You've honored your son admirably, Tony. I can only imagine the pain you must feel losing Kevin."

Tony motioned for Nick and Maureen to take a seat next to his desk, where a scrapbook lay open. Beside it, the newspaper article concerning Professor Mathison's death was cut out and ready to be pasted onto the sterile paper.

Watery eyes looked into theirs and a quivering voice began to tell details of his son's life. "Kevin was everything that ever mattered to me. We faced the world together from the time he was an infant. He lost his mother in a car accident on the way home from the hospital two days after he was born. As you can see," Tony gestured with his hand to the wall, "he was gifted with not only an athletic ability, but intelligence as well. He was on the Dean's list and had his heart set on working with NOAA. Got a letter over there accepting him into their graduate program as soon as he got his diploma."

Maureen took a packet of tissues from her purse and handed one to Tony as she dabbed at the wetness on her own cheeks. "I lost a child, too, Tony. I know you feel as though your heart's been ripped out."

"It might have been easier to take if he'd been in some sort of accident, but to have him take his life makes no sense to me. Now, six weeks later, the professor who taught him is dead." Tony turned his attention to Nick. "I guess you'll have your work cut out for you looking for his killer since there isn't a crime scene."

Nick reached into his pocket for his check book. "Oh, there's a crime scene. And yes, we're hard at work on it." Anxious to get on with business, he asked, "Do I make this out to you, or your company?"

"Either one will be fine. Let me give you a receipt, and then I can brief you on the fundamentals of scuba diving."

* * *

After an hour and a half of listening to Tony explain the basics of scuba diving, including the equipment needed, proper breathing techniques, and safety rules, the two novice divers were ready for a break. On the drive home, they chatted about what they had learned. After exhausting that subject, a few moments of silence caused Nick to glance at his passenger. She stared ahead as if her mind was in another zone and Nick asked, "Something wrong? Was it something I said?"

Maureen reached over and touched his arm. "No, not at all. I was just thinking about Kevin. Tony didn't tell us the whole story."

Nick's eyebrows raised in question. "Really? Wait a minute. What do you know that I haven't heard?"

"For all Kevin's achievements, he had a dark side. When we did his autopsy, a toxicology test was taken."

"And?" Nick rushed in.

"The results showed his system was loaded with cocaine."

"No! What a shame!" Nick shook his head in disappointment. "Why do these young people who have every advantage screw up their lives with drugs? I can't tell you the number of times I've lectured Penny."

Maureen's voice softened. "Nick, how many of us in AA messed up with alcohol? It's life. We don't always know the reason."

"Good point. Kevin may have been living on his father's pedestal, and that's a hard place to be. So drugs could have played a part in Kevin's suicide along with the toxic gases he mixed."

"My guess is the cocaine gave him the confidence to follow through on his plan."

"Wow, that piece of autopsy news must have shattered Tony's image of his son."

Maureen took the conversation in another direction. "He may have known Kevin was taking cocaine and a confrontation triggered the suicide."

"Hmm," Nick's lips pursed in a thin line that always indicated serious thinking. "Good point. Now the sixty-four thousand dollar question is where did he get the stuff—on campus or off?"

With a teasing smile, Maureen said, "Looks to me like you have another rabbit to chase, Lieutenant."

Sylvia Melvin

Chapter Seventeen

Brock's left hand, covered in dirty diesel oil, wiped drops of perspiration from his moistened forehead as he replaced an overdue filter on one of the boat's engines. He looked up to see Joe, his cafeteria buddy, coming toward him.

"Hey, man, what's up?" he called over the throaty roar of the engines.

Joe removed his cap and waved it in front of him. "Sure is hot down here. Guess I lucked out getting a job on deck. What'cha doin'?"

Brock picked up the old filter, covered in brownish sludge, and threw it in the trash can. "Can't say much for the former maintenance done on this engine. Things like this can lead to major problems."

"Actually, Captain sent me down here to make sure the engines are running top notch. He noticed a drop in power, and since we're making a run to pick up the goods today, we need all the speed they'll give."

"So today's the day, is it? What's my part?"

"I'll let you know when to come up on deck. You'll start with lookout."

"Tell me what I'm supposed to see. You mentioned before they use subs these days."

Joe eagerly explained, "It will be made of fiberglass, painted blue for camouflage, and can be anywhere from 40 to 60 feet long. They travel barely under the water and have exhaust pipes sticking up."

"How are they powered? Turbo diesel?"

"Yep. Three hundred and fifty horse-powered engine. Travels about eleven miles per hour. Carries a crew of four. Cramped quarters."

Brock let out a deep breath before he continued, "Can't say I'd trade places with them."

"Those guys are paid well to make a run. Some of the subs carry a cargo worth $400 million on the street. It's dangerous business but they're smart dudes. Often, instead of a self-propelled ship, a semi-submersible is used. A ballast tank keeps it about 90 feet submerged while it's being towed by a regular fishing boat. If a patrol ship is spotted—" Joe interrupted his own story and his eyes fixed on Brock's. "That's part of your job. A torpedo-like cargo container is released. It automatically shoots out a buoy that may look like floating debris—maybe a log or somethin'. Inside is a transmitter system for a second fishing vessel to retrieve it and carry on with the delivery. Ain't nothin' suspicious about it." Joe laughed. "Same thing they use on tuna fishing nets."

Brock took a rag and wiped his hands. "Can't wait to see this operation in action. So give me a shout when it's time."

Joe gave one more instruction. "Pick up a pair of binoculars from the bridge. You'll need 'em." He was half-way out the door when he turned and said, "Oh, while I was in the galley, cook had the radio on and I heard some news from your ole stompin' grounds. Gulfview, right?"

Brock threw the rag in the trash and nodded his head in the affirmative. "At one time in my life. What'd you hear?"

"Seems a missin' professor at the university showed up dead in a shrimp net last week. You'll never guess where they found his boat."

Brock sensed Joe enjoyed playing cat and mouse with him. *Humor him,* thought Brock. *He's your best source of information on this boat so far.*

"Hey, Joe, the Gulf isn't exactly a backyard pond. Give me a break."

"A toadstool in block 31. Our drop-off point. Now, how's that for coincidence? Could be he stumbled upon the underwater cache. My guess is he was in the wrong place at the wrong time. Like I told you before, things happen beyond the breakers that nobody ever knows." An evil edge to his voice hinted a warning Brock knew he'd do well to heed.

* * *

Salinger despised waiting; he was a man of action. His long fingers drummed the surface of his desk while he waited for Brock to contact him. For several evenings, he'd stayed late at the office in anticipation of hearing the buzz of his cell phone and a text message from Brock. So far, nothing but silence kept him company. He knew putting a mole in the midst of a dangerous situation was risky business. *There's always the chance he'll turn coat and join the other side. I'm not sure I trust him,* thought Salinger.

No sooner did this admission cross his mind when the face of his cell lit up to indicate an incoming text. He adjusted his glasses on his bony nose, picked up the phone, and held it within close vision. Finally, his mole made his first contact! The text was cryptic:

First pick-up today-4:00p.m.Location- somewhere in Gulf. Place and time changes with each pick-up .Submersible sub used for transport into Gulf. Diver on crew boat retrieves cargo.With exception of crew's share, drugs delivered to a toadstool in block 31and stashed underwater.All I know for now.

Salinger responded:

Okay, okay, I need to know who's buying the stuff and what they may know about a Bertram boat seen around that platform.

Brock returned:

May take a while. They're tight-lipped. Remember, I'm the new guy on board. Gotta go.

Salinger, tired but relieved, slipped his phone in his jacket pocket, turned out the light, and headed for home. With his thoughts still wrapped up in Brock's message, Salinger had to admit his mole confirmed what the DEA suspected. *So the drugs are coming in on those home-made subs we've been hearing about. Have to admit it takes guts to hole up in one of those. And the rumor we heard about Blue Boat is true. That toadstool is a hot platform. Still too soon for immediate action—gotta flush out the bigger fish.*

Salinger walked with a strut as his mind visualized a supervisor's job in Operations.

Chapter Eighteen

"**H**urry Dad! The chapel on campus isn't all that big, and I know Professor Mathison's service will be well attended. I hope we can find a seat."

"Coming, honey. I was reading the reports one more time. Megan, his widow, called and wants to meet with me later this afternoon. She seems anxious to talk."

"Poor soul," Penny commented. "If I were in her shoes, I'd be biting at the bit to help find my husband's killer, too."

"Oh, we'll find him. I've never given up on a case yet."

The stream of cars entering the university grounds and heading toward the chapel left no doubt in Nick's mind that his daughter's prediction was right on.

Fortunately, Conner had the presence of mind to have Heather secure seating for the four of them. Soft, calming, spiritual music set a reverent mood. At the front of the chapel and in the center of a lace covered table, sat a silver cremation vase; to the left was a photo of Craig Mathison and to the right an open Bible. On either side stood a single floral stand supporting a large wreath made up of autumn-colored flowers.

Nick, always vigilant, scanned the room for anything suspicious. It wasn't unusual for a killer to show up at a funeral. According to the psychology department, it added another element of excitement to the crime for them. *Morose!* thought Nick as he searched faces. Most of the attendees were unknowns to him, but he recognized a few—Dr. Tindle, college friends of Penny's, a couple of political figures, and Tony Colbert.

Hmm, guess he's paying his respects on behalf of Kevin. Come to think of it, I noticed the article about the professor clipped from the paper on Tony's desk Saturday. Guess he collects anything even remotely connected to his son.

Soon, the service began and accolades from those asked to speak continued for several minutes. Except for sniffling, the occasional cough, or a release of laughter, the atmosphere was one of respect and celebration of a life well-lived.

Since the reverend explained there would be a private scattering of Craig Mathison's ashes on the Gulf waters in the future, no burial service followed.

After a closing prayer, Conner looked at his watch and reached across the pew to Nick. "We've got a couple hours before the meeting with Mrs. Mathison, so why don't we take our gals out to lunch?"

Penny beamed. "Yes! I won't have to cook tonight. How does the Olive Garden sound?"

The hostess at the restaurant seated the foursome at a roomy table, and no sooner had Conner sat down when he noticed Tony sitting alone two tables away. "Hey, let's invite him to join us."

Before anyone could object, Conner was on his feet and in a matter of seconds and then the party increased to five. Tony acknowledged everyone with a greeting and thanked them for the invitation.

"After attending the prof's service, I didn't really feel like going home to an empty house," he explained.

Heather spoke up. "I know it must have been hard on you. Your son was a student of Craig's wasn't he?"

Tony nodded. "He knew Kevin well. They had this diving bond and they actually dove out in the Gulf together a few times. Kevin had his heart set on a marine biology career. He was one course away."

Tony turned to Nick. "How is the investigation moving along? Anything new? This has got to be a tough one."

"Not that I'm at liberty to tell. Of course, I'm sure you know that."

"Oh yeah, just want to see justice for his family and all the students he touched."

"They'll get it. Conner and I will see to that."

As the waitress approached the table to take orders, conversation ceased and images of a delicious Italian meal took precedence.

* * *

Conner and Nick arrived at the Mathison residence at exactly the appointed time. Megan's sister Kathy lead them into the living room where a grieving widow gave them a faint smile and thanked them for coming.

Nick got right to the point. "Mrs. Mathison, we're here to help you through this by answering any questions we can. What do you want to know?"

Megan dabbed at her eyes with a tissue and simultaneously touched the wedding band she now wore on a chain around her neck. "Please start from the beginning, Lieutenant. From the moment you saw Craig's body in the net."

Nick relayed the facts, choosing his words carefully. *There's no need to tell her the Gulf scavengers feasted on his face until it was unidentifiable.* Finally, satisfied he'd covered all the information the Sheriff's Office had, he assured her the case was top priority.

Conner gave his partner a break and asked, "Ma'am, did Craig ever discuss with you the possibility that his life was in danger?"

"I know he was harassed by Harbor Oil." Megan responded. "They were upset that a documentary describing the environmental damage to the Gulf was in the hands of PBS. In fact, Craig turned down a bribe—flatly refused every penny." Megan's chin rose in admiration. "My husband was a man of integrity. He couldn't be bought."

"Not many of those around these days," commented Conner.

"I believe that's one of the reasons his students respected him. You saw the turn out this morning. He wanted them all to succeed and he took it to heart when they didn't. Take that young Kevin Colbert. Tore Craig up when he heard the boy had taken his own life."

Nick entered the conversation. "Actually, I've got a few questions about that that you might be able to shed some light on. Do you mind?"

Megan replied, "Of course not, Lieutenant. Ask anything."

From what Kevin's father tells us, Kevin spent a good deal of time with Craig. Is that so?"

"They both shared a love of diving and Craig took him out on the boat several times. They'd tie up to a platform and check out the artificial reef." Megan paused for

Death Beyond the Breakers

a moment as if reluctant to continue but after a brief second continued. "According to Craig, Tony had high expectations for his son, and although the lad worked hard, there were times he struggled. He admitted to Craig he feared letting his father down."

"We've heard that," offered Nick. "In fact, my daughter sensed the same thing. Kevin hung out with Penny and some of her friends from the biology class."

Megan continued, "Craig suspected Kevin was on drugs the last three or four months of his life. After years of teaching students, Craig got pretty good at spotting the ones who came to class high. Kevin's motivation changed and his work lacked the effort and promise it once showed.

Maureen's words came back to Nick. The toxicology report showed cocaine in his system.

"Did Craig know where Kevin got his drugs? On or off campus?" asked Conner.

"He wasn't sure, but had an idea it was off campus. Kevin told Craig that he had this terrific job during the summer working as a diver for one of the crew boats that service the platforms. My husband suspected they were running drugs from Mexico and delivering to pickup points in the Gulf. I wake up at nights wondering if Craig was killed by some cartel. He could have seen something that cost his life." A new stream of tears flooded her eyes.

Nick prodded deeper. "Was Tony aware that Kevin was involved with drugs?"

A tattered tissue in Megan's hand was now in shreds as she dabbed at the wetness on her cheeks. "Craig got to know Tony pretty well since he was a regular customer at Diving Deep, so he felt he owed it to him to explain the change he'd seen in Kevin's behavior. It bothered Craig that Tony didn't appear to take it seriously. He even acted put out that Craig would make such an assumption. But then you

113

know, parents don't always like to hear anything negative about their children."

For a second, guilt washed over Nick's face and he confessed, "I've been there, done that. Sometimes, as the old adage goes, we can't see the forest for the trees. As parents, we're too close to them. It takes an outsider to show us the truth. Well now, let's get back to the real point of our visit."

Conner, with his pen ready to take notes, asked, "Ma'am, if you can, tell us what Craig planned to do the day he was last seen. Who did he talk to and why did he go out in the boat alone?"

Megan took a deep breath and recalled Craig's activities the last day she saw him. "He wasn't supposed to go alone, but my brother, who planned to go, was called into work. The last conversation I had with Craig was on the phone. He called me from Diving Deep, where he always had his tanks filled, to tell me Mark couldn't go, but not to worry because he'd be fine." Megan extracted another tissue from a box beside her chair.

As much as Nick hated to do it, he reached into his folder and pulled out the threatening note found in Craig's office. "I have to show you something that may be difficult to see, but we need to know if Craig ever discussed this with you." A startled look crossed Megan's face and her hand shook as she reached for the paper. It took a second for the words "Your days are numbered" to register, but when they did, she dropped the note and cried, "No! Where did you get this?"

"It was in a drawer in Craig's office along with copies of the documentary."

"Not once did he mention his life was threatened. Harassed, yes, but nothing like this. Lieutenant, please tell me Harbor Oil is going to be investigated for murder."

Nick looked into her pleading eyes. "Don't worry, Mrs. Mathison, we already have an appointment to meet with their CEO."

Chapter Nineteen

"Gentlemen," a rising tide of red crept up the side of Alex Bowden's broad neck. "Harbor Oil made mistakes on Drilling Rig 24, and we'll be paying for them for years to come—but outright murder? No! As CEO of this company, that's not my style."

Nick raised his hand in an attempt to stop the perception that he and Conner were there to lay blame. "Whoa, sir! We're not accusing you of murder. It would be remiss on our part if we didn't talk to you about your relationship with Professor Craig Mathison. It's no secret he was the lead environmentalist investigating the oil spill."

"And," offered Conner, "the one who filmed the damage, which I've witnessed myself."

"Is it true you made several calls to the professor to dissuade him from offering the film to PBS?" continued Nick.

A slow smirk snaked across Alex's lips. "You've done your homework, Lieutenant. I won't deny it. What he intended to show the public isn't exactly the kind of public relations Harbor Oil needs right now."

"According to our sources, your last communication with him was to offer a sizeable amount of cover-up money. Correct?"

Alex raised his eyebrows in surprise. *That was confidential information. What else do these men know?* he mused. His tone becoming more serious said, "Actually, what we offered was a very generous corporate grant to UWF's Marine Biology Program that would have helped us all work together to mitigate the damage to the Gulf waters and the local economy. Naturally, that grant would likely have generated a considerable bonus to the professor through the university. Mathison was a fool. He could work at that university for the rest of his life and not make what we would channel to him. Yes, the company was disappointed he couldn't be encouraged to partner with us to protect the environment, but once again, let me make it clear...the executives at Harbor Oil do not have a hit list."

A moment of silence heightened the room's tension before Alex shifted the conversation. "However, we have hundreds of employees who depend on this company for their financial survival. If Harbor Oil suffers, so do their jobs."

"What are you suggesting?" asked Nick.

"Someone down the line may have taken the threat presented by Mathison into their own hands. I can't control everyone's behavior."

"So you think, without your approval, one of your men could have taken him out?"

"Just a supposition, Lieutenant. Don't put words in my mouth." Alex squirmed in his over-stuffed swivel chair. "Now, as you may well imagine, I'm a busy man these days. It's one meeting after another and I'm already late." His stocky frame stood up and he offered Nick his hand. "If you have further questions, you know where to reach me."

Both Nick and Conner returned the handshake and thanked Alex for his time with a reminder. "We'll be in touch."

* * *

The hour-long drive from Mobile back to Gulfview, gave the detectives time to mull over the investigation. Conner recited the facts as they knew them.

"So far," he started, "we know the cause of death and that ballistics identified the bullet retrieved from the sofa as a .223 caliber. The unknown fingerprints and blood on the gaff hook could be those of the killer, but remain a mystery. Harbor Oil's offer to buy off Mathison does not bode well for them."

Nick cut in, "Can you imagine the public's reaction if that little tidbit hit the media? Did you notice how uncomfortable Bowden looked when I brought that up?"

"Sounded to me like he was trying to shift the attention off the top brass and sacrifice one of his own. Glad I don't work for him."

"We'll keep an ear to the ground. Something may come of that."

Conner reached over and turned the radio on. "Enough shop talk. My brain needs a rest. Say, how did your first lesson go with Tony?"

Nick stretched his legs out, reclined the seat and yawned. "Not much to tell—mainly classroom stuff. Maureen and I decided to take the fast track and go every night this week to get the preliminaries over. I'm looking forward to the open water dive. That's why we're doing this, right?"

Conner's smug smile preceded his response. "You'll never forget your first dive, partner. I guarantee it."

* * *

After three classroom lessons, Tony decided the fourth lesson for Nick and Maureen should take place in the pool. Eager to use the information he'd learned, Nick arrived early at Diving Deep. Tony was engaged with a customer, so he walked into the classroom and took another gaze at the gallery photos. Since most were taken of Kevin at various stages of his life, Nick was taken aback to see a picture of Tony dressed in a Navy Seal combat uniform carrying a weapon.

At the sound of footsteps, Nick turned to see him enter the room.

"Hey, Tony, didn't know you were once a Seal. Conner never mentioned it."

A hearty laugh rumbled through the room. "It's just a part of my past. When I was young and foolish. Those days are over. Some of the hardest training I ever did. Man, they put us through some tough stuff. I don't know how I survived. I must admit, though, it helped shape my career. I was part of an Underwater Demolition Team—taught me everything I know about diving."

"That's quite a weapon you're carrying," Nick placed his finger on the photo showing the rifle. "What is it?"

"M4A1 Carbine Rifle. About the only thing I took with me when my tour was up. It's locked up over yonder in that spear cabinet."

Nick walked over to see the rifle first hand.

"Goes with me every time I'm out on the Gulf. One can't be too careful, especially if I'm alone. Chances are the professor would be alive today if he'd had one of these on that boat. The paper didn't say, but did he have anything to defend himself with?"

"Not that we found," Nick lied.

"Well, even if he did, there's no way drug running pirates would leave weapons behind. They bring big black market money in Mexico. I'm surprised they left the boat. A Bertram would bring in a nice piece of change."

"Might have been scared off by a patrol boat," Nick suggested.

Tony shook his head from side to side. "Guess we'll never know."

"Never know what, guys?" Maureen, rosy cheeked and a little breathless, entered the room. "Sorry, I'm running a little late. Had to finish a report on a cadaver."

Tony gave her his best smile. "We're just chewing the fat, waiting on a lovely lady."

Nick caught on to Tony's flirtations and walked over to Maureen. "Changing rooms are on the right. Last one in the pool has to buy coffee tonight."

* * *

For the next three sessions, Nick and Maureen met poolside with Tony and learned how to read pressure gauges, attach and remove a regulator from a tank, clear a flooded mask while under water, and swim with scuba equipment while maintaining control of their direction and depth while breathing naturally.

Nick had a problem giving Tony his full attention; his eyes kept meandering over to Maureen, who, although in her forties, looked great in a swimsuit. Not only that, but she caught on to the instructions with no intimidation and swam like she had a second pair of lungs. *She's a natural,* he observed. *Of course the extra attention Tony gives her while I'm struggling to keep up has to pay off.*

It was after the monthly AA meeting, while sitting at their favorite spot at Starbuck's, that jealousy bore it's ugly head. Maureen offered Nick a bit of news.

"Oh," she began, "I ran into Tony at the bank yesterday and he invited me out to lunch."

Nick bristled. His coffee mug slammed against the top of the table, sending brown liquid over the edge. "Oh, excuse me," he stammered, his color deepening as he took a napkin and mopped up the mess. "And did he entertain you with talk of all his diving escapades?"

"Actually, you came up in the conversation, Nick."

"Me?"

"He asked a lot of questions about the professor's investigation. Of course, I didn't give him any specifics, but I did tell him you're a smart cookie and there's no doubt in my mind the case will be solved."

Nick's smile returned.

"Seems Mathison was a regular customer at Diving Deep, and of course there was the connection with Kevin." Maureen sensed Nick's demeanor change and added, "I really think he wanted someone like me, who'd also lost a child, to listen to him grieve. My heart goes out to him. I sense he's a lost soul reaching out for a life-line."

And he'd like nothing better than to have you save him, mused Nick. A sudden chill of disappointment settled over him and dampened the feeling of the bond he felt between them, and with one last swig of coffee, he got up and announced, "I've got an early morning meeting with the sheriff. Time to call it a night."

Chapter Twenty

Finally, the big day arrived—time for the open water dive. Still miffed that Maureen had a soft spot for Tony, Nick took it out on Penny at breakfast.

"I noticed you're not keeping up with the housekeeping duties like we discussed. My bathroom smells of damp towels and there isn't a clean glass in the cupboard."

Penny, guilty, pleaded her case. "Dad, in case you haven't noticed, I've been hard at work studying for mid-terms. We also agreed, my education comes first. I'll get back on track now that exams are over. What's eating you, anyway? You've never obsessed over trivia like this before."

Nick stuck a chunk of toast in his mouth, got up, and opened the overloaded dishwasher. With no place to stick his plate, he dumped it in the sink. "Just got a lot on my mind. I apologize. Say, how 'bout I give you a reprieve and you come watch your ole dad take his first open water lesson today? Conner and Heather are coming." Nick paused. "And Maureen."

Penny gave her dad a hug. "Yes! You mean I finally get to meet this mystery woman. I wouldn't miss it for anything! When do we leave?"

"In an hour. Tony said the boat leaves at ten."

"Dad, can I be your buddy? I'm sure you've learned that's a cardinal rule for diving."

"You bet. I'll give the shop a call and tell them to fill another tank."

* * *

At the dock, an excited group got aboard the Scuba Skipper boat. Nick introduced Maureen to Penny, who gave her father's friend an inconspicuous once-over. *Nice,* she admitted. *I can see why Dad is interested.*

Conner and Nick requested they take their dive at the toadstool where the Bertram was found. They wanted to see first-hand what might have attracted Mathison to that particular platform. The Gulf was choppy, but the Scuba Skipper was a big boat, so the ride was comfortable. As other recreation boats whizzed by, their riders waved. An October sun glistened on the emerald water, sending jeweled beams of spray toppling over each other. A perfect day for an underwater adventure.

After an hour, oil platforms loomed into view, emerging from the depths of the Gulf. The boat's GPS guided the craft to the designated spot and one of Tony's helpers tethered it to the legs of the toadstool.

Nick looked around at the expanse of water on all sides. It wasn't hard to imagine the crime scene on the Bertram happening with no one to witness it.

"Okay, folks." Tony's voice brought Nick back to the present. "Gather round for the briefing. First timers, you have a depth limit of no more than sixty feet. Experienced divers like you Conner are good for a hundred. The first fifteen to twenty feet may be a little murky due to the presence of emulsified oil, thanks to Harbor Oil. After that, it should be clear, and you'll see the artificial reef and an underwater world that will amaze you. If it's too murky, we'll have to dive another day. That mess can really foul dive gear, and it takes forever to clean up. Your buddy's been certified, so pay attention and listen to their instructions. Any questions?"

Maureen spoke up. "I don't have a buddy."

"You're going with me." Tony's gaze lingered longer than Nick thought necessary. "Hey, start to set up your gear. We came to dive."

For the next several minutes, there was little chatter as everyone did a safety check on their equipment, suited up, donned their buoyancy vests, and picked out a colored tank, each individually initialed. Tony entered the water first and waited for Maureen to topple over the side of the boat.

Meanwhile, Conner rechecked Nick and Penny's pressure gauges to be sure each tank held the 3000 pound per square inch capacity. Just as Nick reached for his tank, Penny stopped him.

"Oh, please, Dad, let me have the yellow one. It's my lucky color. You take mine. The blue one."

"Being a little superstitious, aren't you?"

"Maybe...can't hurt, can it?"

"I'm the one who needs reassurance, sweetheart. Don't take your eyes off me."

"We went over the hand signals, Dad. You'll be fine. Remember to inflate your vest and adjust the weights before we start our descent. Since the water may not be clear at first, I'm going to take your hand until it improves."

Once in the water, Nick followed all the procedures he learned in the pool. Somehow, they seemed easier to perform in the larger open water. For the first ten feet, a haze of what must have been oil droplets and wispy curtains of soapy looking water obscured his vision. *No wonder the professor was anxious to get his research out to the public,* he mused. *And, I can see why Harbor Oil would try and stop him.*

Suddenly, everything changed. A kaleidoscope of color appeared in the crystal-clear water. Layers of sculptured coral in variegated shades of purple, green, pink and yellow attached to the platform pilings gave cover for marine life. Streaks of silver flashed before Nick's eyes as schools of fish scurried past. The deeper they dove, the sea fans, algae, and sponges swayed in a dance enticing them closer. For a second, Nick looked above him and silently passing over like a stealth bomber glided a Sting Ray. The wonder of it all mesmerized him and he almost forgot to keep sight of Penny. He knew they were allowed thirty minutes from time of descent to ascend and it was almost time to leave. Glancing to his left, he saw his daughter signaling with a clenched fist against her chest—trouble! She pointed to the Submersible Pressure Gage that tells how much air is left in the tank. Nick saw the pressure dropping. *How can this be happening?* One look at the panic in Penny's bulging eyes sent his heart racing. He looked around for help, but the others were not in sight. *Had he made the mistake of wandering too far from the group? Calm down. Get control. Think.* Muddled thoughts went back to the pool. *Buddy breathing.* He prayed he could remember the procedure.

Get in position. Face your buddy. Signal your intentions to share your regulator. Take three normal breaths. Give the regulator to your buddy and show two fingers. Exhale first to clear the regulator. Establish a rhythm. Begin the ascent.

Nick persevered. He searched Penny's face for clues that his clumsy attempt to save her was working. *She's losing focus.* A father's heart cried out, *Keep breathing, sweetheart. Keep breathing.* At that moment, Nick understood the torment and desperation parents like Tony and Maureen must have experienced in losing a child. Regaining his focus, he reflected upon the fact that if they ascended too quickly, the consequences could be disastrous for both of them. As difficult as it was to slow down, he managed a brief safety stop and prayed, "Dear God, let my child survive."

Nick looked up, and as they emerged through the oil slick, their masks covered in slime, Penny's limp body fell unconscious and the regulator slipped out of her mouth. The weight belt pulled her out of her father's grasp and she sank below the surface. With adrenaline pumping, Nick dove in time to grab hold of her vest and pulled her up out of the water. Without warning, another diver popped up, took hold of Penny, and yelled to the men on the boat to reach down and pull her on board.

Nick recognized Conner's voice and swam toward him. In seconds, both men climbed the boat's ladder, ripped off their masks, and proceeded to strip Penny's gear. By now, the rest of the divers had surfaced. One look at the action on the boat and they knew something was wrong.

"Is she breathing?" gasped Nick? "She ran out of air!"

As Conner placed two fingers on Penny's neck to check for a pulse, he saw only a slight rise and fall of her chest. "Just barely. Did she take in water?"

"Yes. She went unconscious and slipped out of my grasp before I could inflate her vest."

Immediately, Conner tilted her head upwards and started mouth to mouth resuscitation. Emerging from the back of the boat, Heather and Maureen shrieked in horror, "What happened?!" In seconds, their diving gear was strewn all over the boat as they rushed to Penny's side. Maureen took one look at Nick and knew he was in no condition to help. "Let me relieve you, Conner."

Heather yelled at Tony, "Call the Coast Guard. We need help. Now!"

Nick bent down and held his daughter's hand as she struggled for breath. After several attempts to bring her around, a sudden gush of liquid expelled from her lungs and saturated her chest. She began to cough and each time her breathing came in gulps. Maureen checked her pulse again and relief flooded her face. "She's coming around, Nick."

He hung his head as tears streamed down his cheeks. "Thank you, Lord."

Slowly, Penny's brown eyes opened. She saw her father, squeezed his hand and gave him a faint smile. "I'm cold and so tired. I just want to sleep," she whispered.

Maureen's fingers gently brushed strands of stray hair off Penny's forehead and explained, "You body's had a shock, sweetie, and you need to rest. I'm going to cover you with something."

Heather jumped up and came back with a blanket she yanked out of a storage container. At that moment, Tony yelled from the pilot's cabin, "Coast Guard's several miles away involved with a boating accident. Brace yourselves—we're full power ahead." Instantly, the ignition key started the diesel engine and the dive boat lurched forward into the oncoming waves with increasing speed.

Nick sat on the bottom of the boat and cradled his daughter's head in his lap while Maureen and Heather placed cushions under Penny's back and legs. Every so often, Maureen placed her fingers under the blanket and felt for a pulse. Even though it was erratic, it was a positive sign.

Conner and the young assistants gathered up the scattered dive equipment and placed the tanks in their holding area. Troubled thoughts nagged at Conner the more he stared at the yellow tank. *Why did Penny's air supply run out so quickly? I checked the pressure gauge myself and it indicated a full tank. Right now it's on zero. That should never have happened. I'll get to the bottom of this, my friend. I promise you.*

An hour later, the Scuba Skipper docked. As Penny tried to get up, she cried out in pain and fell back down. "It's my legs, Dad. They feel like they're on fire and I can barely move them."

Conner took charge and pulled Nick aside. "She's got the bends. Get her to the hospital and into a decompression tank immediately. I was afraid of this. Heather, call for an ambulance."

In seconds, the color drained from Nick's face. "It's my fault. I must have brought her up too quickly."

Maureen heard the guilt in his voice and she reached out to touch his arm. "Don't blame yourself! If you'd stayed down any longer with her, we might have lost her. I'll ride with you. I have a little pull around the hospital and I'm sure she'll get immediate attention."

"Thanks. I appreciate your concern."

"And I'll pick up any of Penny's personal items," added Heather.

The sound of sirens brought relief to everyone. As they departed the boat, Tony placed a hand on Nick's shoulder and said, "I'm really sorry. I've never had this happen before. We'll find the problem, I can assure you."

Nick looked his instructor straight in the eye and anger burned below the surface of his reply. "You'd better. Because if you don't, I will."

Sylvia Melvin

Chapter Twenty-One

Weaving in and out of traffic, both Nick and Maureen followed the ambulance in their respective cars into the hospital emergency room parking lot. As she exited her vehicle, Maureen called out to Nick. "I've notified the doctor on duty and he assured me his team will get Penny into the decompression chamber right away."

The medical personnel wasted no time in taking the basics—temperature, blood pressure and pulse. A physician trained in decompression procedures explained, "Penny will spend the next six hours in the tank breathing pure oxygen. The pressure in the tank will be increased to correspond to the underwater pressure. Gradually, we'll reduce it until it reaches the water surface pressure. When we've finished, the nitrogen bubbles will be released from her system."

The intense look of worry on Nick's face disappeared when the doctor patted him on the shoulder and said, "Don't worry, Mr. Melino, I'll be here monitoring the whole procedure. I haven't lost one yet."

With a wan smile, Nick thanked the doctor, then bent over the gurney and kissed his daughter's cheek. "Hang in there, baby. You'll be out of there before you know it."

"I love you, Dad," were Penny's parting words before they wheeled her into the tank.

Emotion combined with exhaustion wilted Nick's body and he staggered against a wall.

Maureen sensed he was coming down off the adrenaline rush and she walked up to him and said, "Go home and rest. You can't do anything here. I have reports I'm working on downstairs, so I'll keep check on her progress."

Nick protested, "No way! I can't ask you to do that."

Maureen looked into Nick's tired eyes, paused, and took one of his hands. "What good will you be to her if you're as fatigued as she is? I insist." Once more she chose her words with care, "Forgive me for being candid, but a trauma like this makes us vulnerable. Be strong, Nick, and don't let your feelings lead you back to old habits. Stay away from the Sandspur. You understand what I mean, don't you?"

A wave of emotion washed over Nick and he pulled Maureen into his arms and held her as though she was his life-line.

"You do know you're an angel from heaven, don't you?"

Before Maureen could respond, the sound of voices and the click of heels coming down the hallway separated them. She repeated, "Go home. I'll call if you're needed."

Reluctantly, Nick followed her advice. In thirty minutes, he was home, in bed, and sound asleep.

* * *

The view from Conner's front porch was a mixture of gilded clouds against an orange sherbet sunset that slowly sank into the Gulf. It should have soothed a restless, troubled mind, but the events of the day played havoc with his thoughts.

How did Penny run out of air? Something went terribly wrong. As he pondered all the possibilities, the familiar buzz of his cell phone brought him back to the present.

"Conner Andrews."

A maturing voice responded, "Seargent Andrews, this is Chris Randall. I was on the Scuba Skipper with y'all today. How is Penny?"

The young man's face grew into focus. "Hi Chris. Nice of you to ask. Well, she's in decompression now, but should be out in a couple hours. We'll know more then."

"Sir..." Chris hesitated and there was a moment of silence before he spoke.

"Yes," urged Conner.

"Sir, one of my jobs at the shop is to clean and maintain the tanks after a dive. When I got to the yellow tank, something was wrong."

Conner perked up and hung on the young man's every word.

"What do you mean, Chris? Wrong?"

"The O ring was missing. She never had one, and that's the strange part because I replaced every tank with a new one yesterday."

Conner nearly dropped the phone. Yes, that would do it. With no O ring, a slow leak would develop and she'd never know it.

"Does anyone else know this?"

"No sir. Tony's gone home and I just finished up."

"Chris, I'm going to ask you to keep this quiet for now. Can I count on you? We may be talking serious business here.

"I kinda was thinking the same thing, Sergeant. That's why I called you."

"Are you on a smart phone now?"

"Yes, sir."

"Chris take several pictures of the spot where the O ring should have been. Also make sure you get a shot of the entire tank with 'Diving Deep' printed on the side. Got that? Either save them on a disc or email them, but get them to me ASAP. The higher the resolution of the pictures, the better."

"No problem, sir."

"You made the right move," encouraged Conner. "Now pretend you never saw a thing and go about your daily chores, okay? I appreciate your call, and if you need to talk again, don't hesitate."

"I won't, sir. Good night."

Conner sat back in his lounge chair and watched the creeping darkness swallow up the last rays of the sun. He reviewed the conversation with Chris over and over in his mind. *Perhaps Tony's helper had inadvertently missed replacing the O ring. Mistakes happen. In any case, Nick needs to know.* Conner's fingers punched the memorized number and waited for his partner to answer.

* * *

After a three hour nap and a shower, Nick felt renewed energy and a gnawing in his stomach reminded him he hadn't eaten since breakfast. *I'll pick up something in the hospital cafeteria,* he decided. *Looks like I'll be there all night.*

A familiar Gator jingle on his cell phone jarred his thought process and he stared at it, almost paralyzed, afraid to answer should it be bad news. Seconds later, reason prevailed and he flipped up the cover. Weak vocal cords uttered, "Hello."

Relief washed over him as he recognized Conner as the caller.

"Nick I have something interesting to tell you. Chris, the young man on the boat today called me a half hour ago."

"I hope he has some explanation." The volume of Nick's voice increased and Conner recognized a hint of anger.

"Stay calm, partner. What I'm about to tell you is sure to light your fire."

Conner relayed the conversation between him and Chris. "I'm trying not to jump to conclusions, Nick. We're trained to look for the facts and that's what we have to do."

"Oh, yeah, well here's a fact partner—someone put my daughter's life in danger and it's a *fact* that I *will* find out who did it!"

Chapter Twenty-Two

Satisfied that Penny was on her way to recovery, Nick kissed her forehead as he prepared to leave the breakfast table and head for work. It was no secret that he'd silently prayed over and over that she would emerge from the decompression tank with no lasting injury.

Penny answered another unspoken prayer Nick hoped for when she said, "I can't believe Maureen stayed with me the whole time." The sincerity in her voice caught Nick by surprise. "She's awesome, Dad. I really like her."

A grin tickled Nick's lips, then spread into a full-fledged smile. "That makes two of us. Take it easy today. See you later."

* * *

The ringing of Nick's office phone jarred him out of a thought as persistent as a leach. *Why was one tank without an O ring? Diving Deep has a reputation for meticulous safety standards. Had Chris been distracted and skipped the yellow tank? Or, was that tank placed in with the others intentionally?*

After the third ring, Nick dismissed the possibilities and picked up the phone.

"Lieutenant Melino."

"I always knew you'd amount to something, Melino. You were the smart one."

Taken aback, Nick racked his brain to identify the caller. The voice sounded vaguely familiar—a long lost friend, college roommate, high school buddy?

Then he remembered. Brock Hamilton! Of all people!

"Well, I'll be..."

"Surprised ya, huh?"

"To say the least—what's it been? Thirty, forty years since we last spoke? The last I heard, you were doing a little time. How can I help you?"

"Actually, I was thinkin' of helping you."

Nick's inner self sprang to full alert. "Really? How's that?"

Brock took a deep breath and proceeded to bring his old football teammate up to date on his latest escapade.

"So, you're Salinger's mole. Don't think he'd be pleased to know we're talking. We have our differences."

"Figured that. He's one of those agents who work just inside the law. I'm plannin' on pullin' a fast one on him. You don't know how many nights I laid awake lookin' at those bars hopin' I'd get a chance to get back at the DEA. Well, here's my chance. I'm hopin' you'll cooperate."

"Whoa! Hold on, Brock. I'm not about to get my neck in a noose. Remember, you're talking to an officer of the law."

Brock's voice took on an edge. "Still the moral soul I knew in high school, eh, Nick? What I'm going to tell you ain't gonna get you in trouble. Just listen. The bottom line is that I'm not going to help Salinger do anything, but I've got some critical information that law enforcement needs. And there's little time to act upon it." An uneasy tremor erupted in Nick's stomach and his body temperature rose as he braced for the worst.

"I told Salinger that the Blue Boat delivers to a toadstool, but our next pick-up is the largest we've ever hauled. Something like 3000 pounds of cocaine. That's too much stuff to stash underwater. So we're coming into Gulfview under pretense that the boat's got engine trouble."

Nick's grip on the phone grew tighter.

"That's your territory, Melino. I'll give you the time and place. Not only will you nab the crew on board, but the guys who normally get the stuff from the platform by boat will be there in vans. Have your guys in position and it'll be like taking candy from a baby."

"Hmm..." Nick finally exhaled and started to reply, but Brock wasn't finished.

"Now here's the kicker. Salinger thinks this delivery is still happening at the toadstool, the usual drop-off. I told him to have patrol boats ready to pounce." A coarse, sneaky laugh followed. "Another Blue Boat will arrive instead about the time our boat docks in Gulfview. His sting operation is going to fall flat. All the action is going to be in your court, Melino."

"Why are you doing this? What's in it for you?"

"Payback for all the hits you took from me on the field, friend."

Nick cringed at the affectionate term friend. "We aren't exactly buddies, Brock. How do I know you're not setting me up?" He thought, *Now, that is the old Brock I knew.*

Brock's tone became agitated. "Look, this is the way it's goin' down whether your boys are there or not. Ignore what I'm tellin' you or turn me into Salinger, and you'll send 3000 pounds of drugs onto the streets. Your choice."

"Ahh...Brock, you were once part of the problem. Are you telling me after three years in prison you've walked out of there a reformed man?"

"Let's just say it's my last patriotic act for the country. I was proud to be a Marine for six years, but I'm jumpin' ship. Literally. My cousin's goin' to scoop me out of the Gulf the minute I hit the water. With three Yamaha 150 hp motors on the back of his boat, I reckon we'll have no trouble getting' to Mexico."

"Skipping the country, huh?"

"That's my plan. Now give me your cell number. I'll be textin' you soon with the date and time. Think it over, Melino. We both win."

Nick reminded Brock, "You know I could call DEA and get them involved. Same result. Drugs seized—crew apprehended."

"What? You don't think Santa Rosa County's Sheriff's Office can handle it? Thought the narcotics department was pretty good. Kept me on the run. Besides, I told you I have a vendetta against DEA—don't want them getting credit for closing down this toadstool operation."

"There's one thing I will promise you, Brock."

"What's that?"

"Since I'm not the head honcho around here, I'll talk to Sheriff Kendall and he'll make the decision."

Brock conceded, "Fair enough. Now give me your cell number."

* * *

An hour later, Nick, Conner, and Trevor Owens, head of narcotics, met in Sheriff Kendall's office to discuss the feasibility of Brock's plan.

A hush fell over the group as each man deliberated in his mind the correct course of action. If they blew it off as a prank and it turned out to be true, the Santa Rosa's Sheriff's Office would miss an opportunity that seldom falls in the authority's laps.

Sheriff Kendal broke the silence with his decision. "We'll do it. If Hamilton's not lying, it'll be the largest drug bust this county has ever seen. If he is," Kendall looked at Owens, "we'll consider it a practice maneuver for your boys, Trevor."

"What about Hamilton? What do we do with him if the raid goes down?"

Nick spoke up, "He'll be headed for Mexico before the crew boat even docks. And personally, I don't care if he drinks tequila and listens to mariachi music the rest of his life. For once, he played ball on the right team."

"Owens, you stay here and we'll start some preliminary planning," said the Sheriff. "Melino, let us know as soon as Hamilton gets back to you. My adrenaline's pumping already at just the thought of bustin' up that operation!"

* * *

Attending AA meetings took on a new perspective for Nick now that Maureen accompanied him. A growing bond between them gave him the confidence needed to speak candidly and without reservation.

While sitting at their regular table at Starbuck's, Nick made a confession.

"I'm having nightmares since the diving incident. I wake up in a sweat reliving those moments when I thought I'd lost Penny." Fear in Nick's eyes prompted Maureen to place a hand on his arm." The temptation to erase the memory with a case of Bud is almost more than I can handle."

Maureen gave Nick a straight answer. "Temptation will always be there, especially at a rough time in your life, but you can learn to resist it. I'm not saying it's easy. Remember, I've been there, too. Choose one of our twelve steps when you feel yourself slipping and let it become your mantra."

Nick gave his companion a weak smile, squeezed her hand and continued his confession. "I went to see the department's shrink today."

Maureen drew in a sudden breath and her emerald eyes widened in surprise. She cut Nick off, her voice filled with alarm. "Oh, no, you don't need a psychiatrist, Nick. What you're experiencing is perfectly normal."

A chuckle from Nick eased the tension. "No, no...not for me. Of course, I may need one before this is all over. But it's something else that's part of my nighttime problem. I've racked my brain trying to understand why one of the tanks was tampered with. Who did it? I have a suspicion and I needed some answers from an expert who understands human behavior."

"You aren't going to tell me the details, are you?" The teasing smile and sparkle returned to Maureen's demeanor.

With tongue in cheek, Nick replied, "Pride, my dear. If I'm wrong, I wouldn't want to spoil the illusion you have of my perfect record."

Maureen drained her coffee mug, observed the smug expression on Nick's face. "We're all entitled to one mistake, aren't we?"

Nick leaned closer to Maureen's ear as he helped her on with her coat and lowered his voice. "Let me tell you a secret. I reached my limit a long time ago. I can't afford to get careless. With any luck, tomorrow may be the day I've been waiting for."

Chapter Twenty-Three

The smell of burnt toast and the sound of hissing bacon shriveling up in a pan on the stove caught Penny's attention the moment she entered the kitchen. She looked for her father, who'd abandoned his breakfast, and found him rummaging through a basket he kept on the cupboard to house his keys, pens, bills, and other odds and ends.

"Wow! exclaimed Penny. "Whatever you're looking for must be important 'cause food is certainly not a priority this morning."

Nick turned a few degrees to his right and acknowledged his daughter. "Mornin', baby. You're right. Somethin' else on my mind. You didn't happen to see a receipt from Diving Deep laying around, did you? I need it bad." Nick continued to pull out a handkerchief, a name tag, and an expired pizza coupon.

"Dad, you paid Tony almost a month ago. Heaven only knows where it is. That was always a pet peeve of mom's." Penny's voice took on a nagging imitation of her mother's complaint. "Nick Melino, you'd lose your head if it wasn't screwed on!"

"Thanks, sweetie. Just what I needed to hear to start my day." Seconds later, a victory sigh signaled the end of Nick's search. "Caught on the side of the basket."

"So what's so important about your diving lessons receipt? You and Tony have a financial disagreement?"

Nick reached in and carefully dislodged the stuck paper with a pair of tweezers, then deposited it into a baggie.

"Wish it was as simple as that. If my hunch is correct, I'll be paying my diving instructor a visit. And it won't be a social one."

Nick took a quick glance toward the stove. "Take care of that bacon grease for me, sweetheart. Gotta run. I'll pick up an Egg McMuffin on my way. Love ya."

* * *

The smell of freshly brewed coffee luring the staff into the break room did not deter Nick from his mission this morning. He walked past and went into his office toward the file cabinet. After thumbing through the files, he extracted the one marked 'Mathison - Homocide' and placed it on his desk. Sitting down, he leafed through the pages until he found the prints taken off the gaff hook and the threatening note hidden with the Harbor Oil research CD's. For the second time this morning, Nick took a pair of tweezers, plucked the note from the folder, and deposited it into a second clear plastic bag. He focused his thoughts on the material before him. *Was there a connection? Would prints off his diving receipt match the others?*

A comment made by the department psychiatrist gnawed at him all night and spawned his present actions.

"Losing a child by suicide is enough to cause a person's mind to snap. Guilt haunts them and they want revenge. They'll take it out on anyone they feel is responsible for their child's death."

Anxious to test his gut feeling, Nick gathered the baggies and finger prints and headed for the print lab. On his way, he met Conner and the young man who'd been on the diving excursion.

"Mornin', partner. You look like a man on a mission."

"I am," answered Nick. "Got to get over to the lab before they're too swamped to match some prints for me." He glanced at the younger man. "Good to see you, Chris."

"He brought us photos of the yellow tank," said Conner. "Drop by my office as soon as you can. You'll want to see them."

"I will. Got some questions for you, Chris."

Concern crossed Chris's face. "Hope I'm not in trouble, sir."

"No, no, nothing like that, son. See you shortly."

Once in the lab, Nick explained to a technician, "Take prints from the contents of these bags and then compare them with these prints in this folder to see if they match."

"Sounds as though you're hot on someone's trail, Nick," replied a female with a tease in her voice.

"Let's just say if these prints match, I'll have the noose around his neck."

"Well, in that case, I'll get right on it and we'll see if we can tighten it."

Nick chuckled. "You're my kind of gal, Sandy."

A smile revealed a cute dimple in her cheeks. "Be back at five, fingerprints don't lie."

Before stopping at Conner's office, Nick slipped into the lounge and was pleased to see the coffee pot was still half full. After pouring a cup, he turned to leave when Sheriff Kendall came up to him and asked, "Heard from Hamilton, yet?"

"Not a word. Should be soon."

"Well, we've worked out a plan, so let me know the minute he calls. There'll be some men in boats standing by when they start unloading as well as the ground agents. Need to catch 'em in the act."

"You concerned about the DEA?"

"Not really. This is our turf. If this goes like I'm hoping, I'll give them a call and they can come get rid of the stuff." Kendall turned away, then stopped and asked, "Say, how's that Mathison case shaping up?"

Nick swallowed a mouthful of coffee and said, "We might have a break today if my hunch is correct. All depends on the lab results."

Kendall gave Nick an encouraging smile. "Your hunches have paid off in the past, Nick. Let me know how this one works out."

"Will do, boss."

* * *

Conner and Chris were bent over a computer monitor inspecting a set of photos. At the sound of Nick's footsteps, Conner looked up and handed the tool to Nick.

"There's no question about it, the O ring is missing. Take a look."

Nick scrutinized the photo and asked Chris, "You are absolutely sure you replaced it the day before the dive."

"Yes, sir. I take my job seriously. I know what can happen if air starts to leak from the tank."

"Who else has access to the tanks?"

"Tony." Chris hesitated and his voice quivered, "Well, so did Kevin, but you know what happened to him."

"So just the two of you now?" Conner continued the questioning.

Chris regained his composure. "Yes, sir."

"Do you go out on the boat with Tony on all his diving excursions?" asked Nick.

"That's part of my job, too. But every now and again Tony goes off by himself. Especially after Kevin's death. Said it gave him some peace."

"Chris, we need your cooperation." Nick looked into Chris's bewildered face. "Please keep this visit and conversation to yourself. Tell no one. Understand?"

"Yes, sir. My boss is in trouble, isn't he?"

"That's yet to be proven, but it's a possibility."

* * *

Conner waited until Chris left and then he spoke up. "About the Mathison case—you've got a suspect in mind, don't you? You gonna let your partner in on your suspicions or do I have to wait for the movie?" The edge in Conner's voice caught Nick off guard.

"Hey, I'm not trying to play the hero. We've never worked like that. This case is complicated by a number of factors. The murderer could be a hit man for Harbor Oil, which is hard to prove since no one is talking. Then again the professor may have been shot by a drug runner who is probably hiding out in the jungles of Central America, in which case we'll never nab him. A couple nights ago I laid awake thinking about this case and it hit me that maybe we need to start looking locally. Grab your jacket. We're going to pay the Red Cross a visit."

"Wait a minute." Conner raised his hand in defiance. "I don't give blood. I know I've seen my share in this job, but it's a whole different story when they stick a four-inch needle in you and watch your life sustaining plasma drain out of your arm."

Nick snickered. "C'mon, you wimp. There's probably nothing but water in those veins anyway. If you want my take on this murder you're going to have to listen to me in the car."

* * *

The moment the two detectives settled into the vehicle, Nick relayed his suspicions to Conner. "You know I couldn't tell you in front of Chris this morning what I was carrying over to the lab."

"So what was it?"

"The note we found in Mathison's desk drawer, the prints off the gaff, and my receipt from Diving Deep."

Conner's eyebrows knit together in a puzzled frown then reality hit him. " Diving Deep...you mean Tony! Nah. The guy just lost his son, Nick."

"Remember the day you introduced Maureen and me to him? After you and Heather left, he took us into his back room and showed us all of Kevin's awards, photos, and accolades throughout the boy's life. It's like a shrine in there. I noticed an open scrapbook with the newspaper picture and article of Craig Mathison's death cut out and ready to be pasted into the book. I thought that rather strange." Nick glanced over at Conner and saw him nod in agreement. "A week or so later, we were waiting for Maureen and I saw a photo of Tony on the wall dressed as a Navy Seal with a M4A1 carbine rifle propped against a knee. He told me he was an Underwater Demolition Tech and learned everything he knows about scuba diving from his military service. Now we know from ballistics that the bullet we found fits that type of weapon. In fact, Tony has it locked in a case with his spear guns."

"So why are we going to the Red Cross?"

"The day we met, he apologized for keeping us waiting because he said the Red Cross called to ask for a blood donation."

"Yeah, I do recall that part of the conversation."

"We need to confirm his blood type. The gaff showed two different ones—O positive and AB positive, which is rare. Maureen confirmed that Mathison's was the common O positive."

"Hmmm." Conner's mind shifted into detective mode. "So if the prints off your receipt match the ones on the gaff and his blood type is AB positive, we'll have enough evidence to warrant bringing him in for questioning."

"Atta boy. These past ten years we've worked together haven't been a waste after all," needled Nick. "And if the prints we get off the note match with the receipt, he'll be looking at more than questioning. An arrest and DNA typing will be more like it."

"It looks bad for him on the O ring episode, too, doesn't it? Why would he try such a stunt on us..." Conner's mind raced to a conclusion. "Unless he thought we were getting too close."

Nick cut into Conner's thoughts with his suspicion. "You own your tank, so it must have been me Tony was after. But Penny switched tanks at the last minute, and he and Maureen were already in the water. Come to think about it, Tony's been asking some pointed questions about the investigation. He even took Maureen out to lunch, and now I know why."

Twenty minutes later, the two detectives walked into the Red Cross Clinic and asked to see a supervisor. After a short wait, a man in his sixties, stocky and gray-haired, introduced himself as Jonathan Clyde.

"Lieutenant Melino and Sergeant Andrews," said Nick as the obligatory handshakes were made. "May we speak in private?"

"Come on back to my office, gentlemen. What can I do for you?"

"Mr. Clyde," Nick began, "I understand the Red Cross is not allowed to divulge a blood donor's type unless they're given the client's permission. Correct?"

"Yes, sir. I'd lose my job. Been here twenty-seven years."

"However," Nick reminded the supervisor, "if a judge decides there's probable cause, he can over-ride that privacy privilege, and I can deliver a warrant to obtain the information."

The muscles around Jonathan Clyde's lips tightened and a pallor washed over his face before he spoke. "It's happened a time or two. My administrators don't like it. It's hard enough to get folks to give blood, especially if they know their privacy can be compromised."

Nick gave his partner a quick glance. Conner's face reddened as he lowered his eyes in guilt and remembered Nick's chiding him about donating blood.

"I understand," continued Nick, "each donor has a card identifying their blood type."

"That's right. We encourage everyone to have it in their possession. Never know when an accident might happen."

Nick was on a roll. Conner knew better than to break into his partner's train of thought, so he sat back and listened as Nick continued. "Will you look up on your computer the number of AB positive donor calls made on November 14th of this year?"

The room went silent except for the sound of crunched keyboard keys on Mr. Clyde's computer. The moment the data appeared on the monitor, he turned it toward the detectives. Both men leaned forward to get a better view.

"Thirty-five calls were made and seven messages left."

At the top of the page, subtitles separated by vertical lines caught Nick's and Conner's attention. They focused their eyes on donor's name, blood type, phone number, address, date, and time. Number three donor on the list caused both detectives to take out their notepads and write Tony Colbert, AB positive, 850-424-2562, 1500 Pelican Lane, Gulfview, Florida 32507, November 14, 2012, 10:00 a.m.

Nick's body position changed and he sat up with an air of authority. "Mr. Clyde, it's imperative that our meeting be kept strictly confidential. If I need to get a subpoena to find out Tony Colbert's blood type, I can and will." His eyes remained fixed on the man across from him, who developed a nervous twitch on his upper lip.

"I...I can't lose my job." The man was close to shaking.

Conner reassured him. "You notice we didn't ask for a specific name—only the calls that were made on November 14th. As Lieutenant Melino explained, if we need a copy of that information or our suspect's blood type, we'll be back with a warrant."

The detectives thanked him for his cooperation, shook his sweaty hand, and left him pondering his future.

* * *

Although Nick had other cases that required attention, his mind kept returning to the Mathison murder. They'd made a huge leap forward this morning with the blood typing and his breathless prayer was that the lab would match all the prints. Like the old axiom 'a watched kettle never boils,' Nick finally decided 'a watched clock never moves.' Each time he glanced at the one on the wall, he swore it must have stopped. *Will five o'clock never get here?*

While drumming his fingers on the top of his desk, his cell phone blared out the Gator Swamp jingle. In an instant, he flipped up the cover and spoke, "Lieutenant Melino."

The response was short and curt. Nick recognized the caller as Hamilton. "Wednesday night. Ten o'clock. The pier at Marine Industrials. Three trucks disguised as moving vans will be waiting. Hasta la vista, Melino."

The connection went dead before Nick had time to respond. However, his reaction was swift. He switched to his desk phone and dialed the Sheriff's extension. Kendall picked up on the second ring.

"Sheriff, Melino here. Just heard from Hamilton." Nick relayed the vital information.

"Marine Industrials, huh?" said Kendall. "Not too populated around there. Probably a good thing. I expect resistance from these lowlifes, and we don't need the public in the way."

"Sounds as though Wednesday night is shaping up to be pretty interesting."

The inference in the Sheriff's reply sent a direct message to Nick. "Stay out of it, Melino. We'll let Narcotics handle this one. It could get nasty and I need you in Homicide."

Nick had the last word. "Nail 'em, boss. Putting one operation in the Gulf out of business is a drop in the bucket, but eventually the bucket gets full. Be careful. Those boys play for keeps."

Nick leaned back in his chair, cupped his hands together behind his head, and let his thoughts drift as he waited...and waited...for a call from the lab.

Even if the prints all match and the blood types are all the same, there's one last procedure we need to pursue if the evidence has a chance of standing up in court. Without DNA taken from Tony, a smart lawyer can argue that although Tony's blood type is rare, there are others with AB positive and the Red Cross information could be a coincidence. No, a mouth swab needs to be taken.

At 4:45 p.m., Nick got the call from the lab.

"C'mon over and let me show you the results," Sandy urged. "You're right on track as usual. All the prints match."

"Yes!" cheered Nick. The triumphant tone in Nick's response solicited a laugh from Sandy.

"Thought this news would make your day."

"It made mine for sure! Not too good for my suspect. We'll be bringing him in for questioning tonight."

Nick did not linger at the lab. He stayed long enough to have Sandy brief him as they examined each set of fingerprints, then he walked to Conner's office.

"Grab your jacket. I'm ninety-nine percent sure we've got Mathison's killer."

Conner looked up from his computer and gave his partner a thumbs up. "Paydirt! Tony Colbert! I'm still in shock."

Nick pulled out his cell phone and speed-dialed the court house number. "Hope we're not too late to get a warrant." After a brief explanation to the clerk, Nick thanked him, slipped his phone back into his jacket pocket, and with Conner close on his heels, headed toward the parking lot.

Picking up a warrant from a judge was routine for these detectives, but every time one was needed, Nick knew there was a possibility it could be denied.

There shouldn't be any delay today, he mused. *Not with these prints as evidence. Just cause if I ever saw one.*

Chapter Twenty-Four

Tony Colbert finished securing the rope from the Scuba Skipper to the pier and hopped back on board to pick up his gear when the slam of two car doors caught his attention. Walking toward him were Conner and Nick. Their hurried pace and somber facial expressions indicated to Tony that this was no casual social call.

Doesn't look good, he thought and his mind raced as he leaped from the boat and closed the gap between them. *Somethin's wrong.*

Despite his intuition, he welcomed the men with a smile and a handshake. "Howdy, fellas. Whatcha' up to? By the look of those sport jackets, you're not here for a dive." His attempt at levity fell flat.

Nick wasted no words. "We need to talk, Tony. Close up your shop."

"Hey, wait a minute...if this has anything to do with your daughter and that faulty tank, I've no idea what happened. That tank was good to go."

Conner was quick to step in, "That's another issue. Right now we have a warrant for your arrest."

Before Conner could continue, an audible gasp escaped from Tony's lips. "Arrest! For what?"

"The murder of Professor Craig Mathison."

Tony's jaw dropped and his eyes grew cold as anger burned behind his façade of surprise and indignation.

"Craig Mathison! You're out of your minds! Craig was a friend. Took a lot of interest in Kevin. Why would I want to kill him?"

"That's what we'd like to know." Nick looked at Conner. "Read him his rights."

Without further adieu, Conner repeated the words he'd uttered hundreds of times to other suspects as he put the cuffs on Tony's wrists. At the same time, Nick called for a patrol car to meet them at 1500 Pelican Lane. Pronto!

While they waited, Tony ranted and raved. "You guys are way off base. Wastin' the tax payers money tryin' to be a hero over some lofty-headed professor who tried to make a name for himself."

Nick heard enough and walked over and got in Tony's face. "Let me give you some advice, Colbert. You keep mouthing off and you're going to dig yourself a hole that the best lawyer in town won't be able to get you out of."

Tony had no chance for retort, as a familiar Santa Rosa County Sheriff's patrol car pulled into the Diving Deep parking lot. Conner opened the door and advised the deputy, "Take him to booking. I expect he'll want to call his lawyer. We'll be along as soon as we tell the young man inside to lock up. He may not be seeing his boss for awhile."

It was no surprise to Chris when Conner and Nick entered the shop. "Hey, what's going on? I heard some commotion, and when the patrol car drove up and you put Tony in the back seat, I couldn't believe it. Is this about the diving accident?"

"A lot more serious than that, but there may be a connection." Conner was careful not to expose too many facts.

Nick went straight to Tony's office and tried the door. He expected it to be locked, but to his surprise, it swung open. The fading light from a small window across the room cast shadows on the wall. Nick strained his eyes to locate a light switch. With added illumination, he found what he sought—the glass case with different types and sizes of spear guns. But to his disappointment, the weapon he needed to locate was missing. Ballistics had the bullet found in the sofa on the Bertram and according to them, it could have come from a M4A1 Carbine rifle. If it matched to this particular rifle, it made their case even stronger. Besides, another set of prints from the gun was more evidence against the owner.

As Nick stared at the display cabinet, his mind returned to the conversation he and Tony had while waiting for Maureen one evening less than a month ago. Nick recalled it went something like this:

"Yeah," said Tony, "this baby goes with me every time I go out on the Gulf. Never know when you'll need it, especially with the drug runners and boat pirates popping up out of nowhere."

Nick now knew where to look. He wasted not a second, but turned heel and almost knocked Conner off balance in his haste to leave the shop.

"Meet me on Tony's boat," he commanded. "Gotta get my gloves out of the car. We may have some new evidence."

Conner turned to Chris. "Do you know if he had anyone coming in for a lesson this evening?"

Chris walked over to the counter and picked up the schedule book, turned to the latest entry and replied, "Doesn't look like it. The last one was two days ago."

"Good. Now why don't you go ahead and lock up? Tony won't be back tonight."

"Sure is something fishy going on around here. Don't guess you guys are going to clue me in, eh?"

"Not yet, son. Believe me, it'll be in the paper soon enough if we do our job right. Keep your eyes open."

Conner's long strides took him to the Scuba Skipper in time to see Nick enter the captain's cabin. Satisfaction was written all over his face when he emerged carrying the rifle. He was careful not to let the weapon brush against his jacket. The last thing he needed was smudged fingerprints.

The day shift at the Sheriff's Office wasted no time in leaving the parking lot, but as Conner and Nick drove in, Deputy Salter stopped and briefed them. Tony was in booking going through the usual procedure. It would take an hour or more before his fingerprinting, photographing, and medical examination would be completed.

"Did he call a lawyer?" asked Conner.

"Yes, but apparently the man is out of town today. Supposed to be on the job tomorrow."

"Good," chimed in Nick. "It's too late to get a judge involved with a bail hearing. Having him spend a night behind bars is the least of my concern. Serves him right!"

Conner gave the deputy a thumbs up sign. "Thanks, Gus. We'll take it from here. Have a good night."

Nick turned to Conner, held up the weapon and stated, "I'm getting this to the lab now. It's been a busy day, pal, so go spend some time with your fiancé before she changes her mind."

"Hmm...lucky if I get to spend five minutes with her lately." Conner sounded miffed. "I'll be the happiest man alive when these wedding plans are finally settled. You'd think we were the first couple to ever get married."

"In Heather's mind you are, friend. Take my advice." Nick chuckled. "Just sit back and smile."

"Oh, I was supposed to tell you the date's been changed to two weeks from Saturday and she's ordered you a white tuxedo. Since the ceremony is on the beach, she thought it'd look good."

"Sounds fine to me. By the way, I'm considering asking Maureen to be my guest."

Conner's face lit up. "Now, that's the smartest thing you've said all day!"

* * *

On his way back from the lab, Nick noticed Sheriff Kendall's office door was ajar and his boss was sitting at his desk studying a piece of paper. Nick knocked, then stuck his head in before he commented, "Working late aren't you?"

Kendall looked up and waved Nick in to take a seat. "Just looking over the last minute details for the drug bust this evening."

"Man, I almost forgot. Been busy this afternoon with the Mathison case."

"Hear you brought in a suspect, eh? Tony Colbert. That's a shocker."

Nick nodded in agreement. "If he requests a bail hearing, I'm confident the judge will deny it based on the evidence. We did our homework."

"I'm sure you did, Nick." Kendall returned to the paper he held in his hand. "Narcotics just gave me their last minute changes. We'll have boats positioned inside the channel and agents stationed at various locations around the pier. Marine Industrials has consented to let us set up a couple of video cameras. We're ready."

"Sounds like a solid plan." Nick rose out of the chair and with an air of optimism said, "Hey, a successful drug bust and a confession from Colbert would make our week now, wouldn't it?"

A slow smile creased the edges of Kendall's cheeks. "I like the way you think, Melino. Talk to you later."

* * *

Penny scurried around the kitchen preparing well-seasoned steak, baked potatoes, and a salad as her father brought her up to date on the day's activities.

"Tony Colbert!" she almost dropped the lettuce. "Dad, whatever made you suspect him?"

"Well, first off—he's only a suspect. He hasn't had his day in court, but the evidence we've unveiled is not in his favor. Why did I suspect our diving instructor? Because I felt it odd that the newspaper article describing Professor Mathison's death was lying on Tony's desk beside a scrap book of Kevin's achievements. Intuition prompted me to ask a few questions of the experts in our psych department. Seems as though some parents will go to great lengths to avenge the death of a child."

"So he hasn't made a confession?"

"The interrogation should start tomorrow, but, no doubt, his lawyer will ask for bail and the judge will have to review our request to deny it."

Nick's voice took on a lighter tone. "I do have some news that will put a smile on your face, darlin'."

Penny placed the steak on the broiler and closed the oven door. "Tell me, tell me."

"Conner and Heather's wedding is in two weeks. On the beach. And I'm wearing a white tux."

"Cool! Sounds like my father's going to steal the show. Need I ask who you intend to be your date? I could make a suggestion."

"If you're thinking of someone with strawberry blond hair, I intend to call her as soon as I devour that delicious aromatic steak."

* * *

Forty-five minutes later, Nick wiped his lips with a napkin, pushed his chair away from the table and leaned over his daughter's shoulder giving her a kiss on her cheek. "Better than any steak house in town, honey. I was ready for a good meal."

"Thanks, Dad, but don't you have something important to do now? As the old axiom states, strike while the iron's hot. The lady may be making plans of her own, you know."

Nick pulled out his cell phone and started to walk toward the patio. "I'm dialing Maureen as we speak."

At the sound of her voice, Nick closed the glass door leading outside and settled into a comfortable chair.

"Maureen, it's Nick. If I'm interrupting your dinner, I can call back."

"No, no. Is Penny all right?" Nick heard a hint of alarm in her voice.

"Oh, she's fine. In fact, better than fine. She just cooked a lip-smackin' steak tonight. No, this is a social call."

"Well, then, I can relax," sighed Maureen. "What's on your mind?"

A nervous tingle ran through Nick's body. "Take a look at your calendar and see if you have any plans for the first Saturday in December. Conner and Heather have decided to have a beach-side wedding and I'm the best man. I'd like to take you as my guest."

As he waited for Maureen's reply, Nick realized he was holding his breath. *Why do women put us through this torture?* Seconds later, he felt his body relax as she gave him her answer.

"I've never been to a beach wedding. I'd love to be your guest."

"Great! I'm already looking forward to it, even though I'll have to suffer through wearing one of those tuxedos and cummerbunds. Oh, well, anything for my buddy. Speaking of Conner, he and I made an arrest today in the Mathison case."

Maureen gasped. "You did? Someone connected to Harbor Oil?"

"This may come as a shock—Tony Colbert!"

"No way! How did you come to that conclusion?"

Nick repeated the facts as he'd told Penny earlier. "The interrogation should begin tomorrow if his lawyer gets back to town. I'd be surprised if he makes bail on the evidence against him. Besides, I picked up what I believe was the rifle Tony used to kill Mathison. Ballistics is checking for a match on the bullet now."

"I know how thorough you work, Nick, but I just thought of something else that might stand up in court."

"What's that?" Nick tried to imagine what it would be.

"Well, since I'm trained to examine bodies, I notice little marks that other folks may miss. Remember, I told you Tony and I had lunch one day. As he was cutting his meat, I noticed a scar on his upper left hand and on the inside of his palm. I asked him what had happened. He told me one of his students was learning to use a spear gun and the guy got anxious and fired it, hitting Tony instead."

Nick came to his own conclusion. "Was it the size a gaff hook would make? That may be why there were two blood types on the shaft of the gaff."

"My thoughts exactly. Be sure to check out his hands when you talk to him."

"I will. We may have to obtain a court order to get a mouth swab to confirm the DNA from the blood on the gaff is his. I doubt he'll volunteer. Then again, I just may get the DNA on my own." Nick paused and thought a moment. "Yeah, that's what I'll do. Should be easy, but that's tomorrow's story.

"You are such a tease, Nick. Be sure to keep me abreast of the details." Maureen paused a moment and her voice mellowed. "Thank you for inviting me to the wedding. I'm marking it in red on my calendar. Good night."

Sylvia Melvin

Chapter Twenty-Five

The headlines in the morning paper sent Nick's adrenaline soaring: "Santa Rosa Scores Biggest Drug Bust on Record!"

According to the story, everything came off as planned. The Blue Boat's crew was apprehended and over 3000 pounds of marijuana and cocaine were seized. Nick scanned the list of names, and as he expected, Brock Hamilton's was missing. *Adios,* thought Nick. *Thanks for the tip. Enjoy the tequila!*

A triumphant air permeated the Sheriff's Office the moment Nick entered the building. Every person he passed in the hallway wore a smile and appeared to have a spring in his step as they greeted him with, "Did you hear the news?"

* * *

The desk phone in Nick's office continued to ring as he juggled a cup of coffee, a muffin, and his keys while trying to open the door. Coffee slurped down the side of his cup, stinging his thumb, as he bounded into the room and reached for the phone.

"Lieutenant Melino. Sheriff's Office."

"Melino, this is Aston Moore. I'm representing Tony Colbert. I understand he's under arrest for the murder of Craig Mathison."

"That's correct."

"My client is requesting a bail hearing. How soon can that be arranged?"

"Of course, the judge makes that decision, but I'm ready to provide our evidence today if the court is free to conduct the hearing. I'll call over there and see what's on the docket for today and if we get lucky, I'll give you a call. Let me have a number."

"So..." Moore paused and Nick knew from experience what was coming next. "You believe you've got a substantial case against my client, huh?"

"We wouldn't have brought him in if we didn't suspect he's guilty." Nick was having no part in this fishing expedition. "Why don't you wait until the hearing and draw your own conclusion. Now, if there's nothing else we need to discuss, I'd like to make that call."

Once again, Nick's connection with Judge Ramsey paid off. A time slot for 1:15 p.m. was confirmed. It gave Nick plenty of time to organize his evidence. A convincing presentation was crucial in denying a suspect bail. And he needed to make one more trip over to Diving Deep. Something else in Tony's office caught his attention.

* * *

Judge Ramsey's decision whether or not to grant bail to Tony was swift and blunt. "After reviewing the fingerprints taken from a note found in Professor Mathison's desk, which in my opinion amounts to a death threat, and seeing that they match your military file prints, I deny your request for bail."

Tony's jaw muscles tensed and his eyes bore into the judge.

Accustomed to such reactions, Judge Ramsey continued. "You shall remain in custody until a trial date is set. In this country, every individual has the right of presumed innocence until proven guilty. Allegedly, you took another man's life. Prosecution will work hard to prove you did and your defense lawyer will try to show a jury they're wrong. Ultimately, Mr. Colbert, the truth always comes out. You're dismissed to Officer Landon."

Nick stepped up to the officer and said, "Take him to interrogation room four in fifteen minutes."

Anxious to get on with the interrogation, Nick set up the eight by ten foot room the way he wanted in advance. Two straight-back wooden chairs and one regular roller type were set away from a table in an arrangement that looked more like a conversation pit. Off-white blank walls offered no distractions. A camera lens disguised as a thermostat viewed the suspect's entire body, capturing his emotional state, while a microphone taped to the underside of the table picked up every spoken word.

Throughout his years of interrogating suspects, Nick came to the conclusion that starting off in a defensive mode rarely brought the results he sought. Treating an individual with congeniality and dignity often caught them off guard and opened up lines of communication as well as dissolving the tension in the room. Thus a carafe of coffee and a selection of soft drinks sat at the far end of the table. A box of tissues and a folded newspaper lay in the center.

Right on time, the door opened and the deputy ushered in a despondent looking Tony and his stylishly-dressed lawyer. Conner followed behind carrying a notepad and a brown envelope. Nick seated Tony directly in front of him in the wooden chair and indicated to Aston Moore to take the other, a foot from Tony's left and slightly behind him.

"Afternoon, gentlemen. Can I offer you a coffee or a soft drink?" The smell of freshly brewed coffee wafted through the air the moment Nick removed the carafe lid and poured himself a cup.

Tony spoke up first. "Black. One sugar."

Moore declined the offer.

"What? No doughnuts?" A sarcastic tone in Tony's voice continued. "Thought there was some unwritten law you guys weren't allowed to drink coffee without a doughnut in your hand."

Conner, sitting behind him ready to take notes, bit his lip in a gesture of disgust. Nick, not wanting to be put on the defensive, laughed, leaned back in his chair, and crossed his legs before he replied, "Sorry, man, my partner ate the last Crispy Cream this morning."

A moment of silence passed and Nick grew serious. He decided to start the conversation between him and Tony on a level playing field. His eyes scanned Tony's rigid frame and drawn facial features. He needed to get his suspect to relax and get into a comfort zone. *We're both parents without partners. That should do it,* he surmised.

"Tony, my daughter knew your son. They took the same biology courses. It's a challenge raising young people without female support, isn't it? I've been divorced for a couple years now. Never know if I'm doing the right thing or giving the advice she needs. I'm always asking myself, "When do I let go and let her make independent choices?""

Tony's eyes softened and he looked at Nick with renewed interest.

"It's been tough for you, hasn't it? Especially, since the suicide. Feelings of guilt, inadequacy keep you awake at night."

Like a cube of ice starting to melt, Tony's body language spoke for him. First, his shoulders lost their stiffness and sagged, as his head leaned forward and he wiped at his eyes.

Nick waited for a response. After a moment of silence, Tony looked at Nick and uttered a plea. "I did everything I could to try to replace the love his mother would have given him. Kevin was my reason for living. He could have gone so far."

"But the last few months of his life a change came over him, didn't it Tony? His dedication to his career waned and there were behavioral issues."

"What do you mean?" Once again, a defensive tone was evident in Tony's inquiry.

Nick got up and reached for the morning newspaper. He opened to the headline, held it in front of Tony, and asked him to read the large black print.

"So, what does this have to do with Kevin?"

"We know that your son worked on this Blue Water boat this past summer and even the occasional weekend these past months. This crew used him to dive and secure drugs at an underwater cache at an unmanned oil platform."

"You can't prove that."

"Yes, we can. Professor Mathison suspected Kevin was on drugs during class. He confronted him and Kevin confessed."

"Dead men don't talk, Melino."

"You're right, but his wife can and she is willing to testify that her husband discussed the problem with her. He cared about his students. In fact, he felt he owed it to you to break his promise of silence to let you know what was going on. He told you Kevin's degree was in jeopardy and his grades were failing, didn't he? But you didn't want to hear that your son was involved with a drug ring, did you? Not your boy."

"I did confront Kevin. And yes, I lost it. Told him how disappointed I was. He promised to quit going out on the Blue Boat. He even went to Mathison and begged him to give him another chance. The professor refused. Why all the questions about my son?" Tony shifted his weight from one side of the chair to the other, not sure what direction Melino was going in.

Nick looked at Conner and nodded. His partner removed a framed eight by ten photo of Kevin and Tony dressed in scuba gear from the brown envelope and passed it across the table. Nick rolled his chair closer to Tony and turned the picture toward him.

A gasp of surprise and a burst of emotion erupted from Tony as he reached for the frame. Tears welled up in his eyes and dropped on the protective glass. "How'd you get...?" The rest of his question faded away as he hugged the photo close to his chest. His body started to shake and a broken man's sobs filled the room.

The look on Aston Moore's face was forlorn. He knew Melino would get a confession, but not before he had his say. "Low blow, Lieutenant. But then you and I work on opposite sides of the fence."

Nick ignored Moore's comment and waited until Tony got himself under control. "You'd do anything for Kevin, wouldn't you, Tony? Even murder!"

Moore interrupted, "You don't have to answer, Tony."

But like a volcano ready to erupt, the hidden anger in Tony couldn't be stopped and rose to the surface. "He drove my son to suicide. Ruined his reputation and deprived Kevin a once in a lifetime opportunity to work for NOAA. Told him there was no way he could write a letter of recommendation. I knew where Mathison was going that morning. He came in to get his tank filled. Told me exactly where the Maritime Explorer was headed. I overheard him tell his wife her brother backed out and he'd be alone. It was the perfect opportunity to take him out."

Nick came back with his own interpretation. " Your first shot grazed his temple didn't it? He still had his faculties and he surprised you with a gaff hook when you put your hand on the back of the boat to hoist yourself onto the deck. Judging from those scars, that's one piece of evidence you'll live with for the rest of your life."

Moore looked closely at Tony's hands and shook his head from side to side in submission. "With your permission, Lieutenant, I'd like to speak to my client."

Nick and Conner rose from their chairs and Nick checked his watch. "Fifteen minutes. I still want some answers."

Instead of standing around waiting for Tony and Moore to finish their conference, Nick walked over to Kendall's office. Since the door was open, he popped in and extended his hand. "Congratulations on a job well done last night. I have to admit, I was a little nervous. One never knows about Hamilton but I guess he really does have it in for the DEA."

"Thanks, Nick. You played your part, too, but speaking of the DEA, I called Salinger, and he's not too happy we participated in the bust. He wanted to know who Hamilton talked to, but of course that's our business, not his. He's ready to string Hamilton up. That is if he ever catches him." Kendall gave a hearty laugh. "Doubt that will ever happen. The Mexicans will protect him."

Nick stole a look at his watch. "Gotta get back to my suspect. He's talking to his lawyer now. We've got a video confession, but I want his signature. My guess they're discussing plea bargaining right now."

"I'll be interested in the video, Nick. Let me know when it's finished."

* * *

Tony's face looked flushed and he paced back and forth. When the door closed and the two detectives took their seats, he settled down again in the wooden chair. This time, Moore took the lead.

"If Tony signs a confession, what are the chances the prosecution will cut a deal? Say a reduced sentence with parole."

Nick despised this segment of the bargaining ploy. He always believed that if a human life was intentionally taken, then the full price needed to be paid.

"So what's your client got to offer?

Moore pointed to the headlines in the paper. How'd you like the name of the kingpins in this Gulf cartel?

Nick's eyebrows shoot up in surprise. "Keep talking."

"Kevin overheard a private conversation on board the Blue Boat."

Tony could no longer keep quiet, his voice shaking, "He let it slip when I confronted him with Mathison's accusations."

"So who is it?" It took some control on Nick's part to keep his voice calm.

All eyes bore down on Tony. Even Moore was sitting on the edge of his seat.

"The owners of the Emerald Lady Casino."

"Figures," chimed in Conner. "The high rollers are a ready market."

"You're right, but hey, our boys got what they were after last night. We'll give this new info to the DEA and see if this dog will hunt, as a wise ole judge in this town used to say. You know the decision comes from the District Attorney's Office. I'll have to give them a call." Nick pulled out his cell phone and dialed. After a short explanation, he was told to bring the defense attorney over in twenty minutes.

"While we're waiting, I have another question I'd like answered." This time, it was personal and Nick's demeanor changed. "Someone sabotaged the O-ring on the yellow scuba tank my daughter used. We have pictures to prove it and a statement from Chris at your shop that he replaced every tank with a new one the day before our dive. I can't believe anyone intended to harm my daughter. I was the target, wasn't I?" Nick watched Tony's eyes dart from side to side, a sure sign of nervous behavior. "Were you afraid our investigation was closing in on you, Tony? By the way, that's another strike against you—attempted murder."

By now, Moore was loosening his fancy tie and looking at his client in disbelief. "What's this all about?"

"I'll tell you on our way to the D.A.'s office," offered Nick.

Tony bent his head and cupped his face in his hands. His whole body appeared to dwindle in defeat.

"I'm waiting for your answer, Tony."

"Yes, it was you, Melino!" His voice rose to a shout. "Your bulldog reputation in this town is well known. I knew it was a matter of time before you fingered me, but if you were out of the picture, I might have a chance. You offered me the perfect opportunity when you joined the scuba class. It might have worked if you hadn't changed tanks with Penny."

"You think my partner, over there," Nick pointed to Conner, "wouldn't have tracked you down?" Nick felt his temperature rising, a sure sign he was close to losing his professionalism. *Better to quit while I'm ahead. He's not worth losing my cool over.*

Conner recognized the signs and knew it was time Nick left the room. "It's going to take you five minutes to walk over to the D.A.'s office, so you two better high tail it out of here. He doesn't like to be kept waiting. Tony, I'll have a deputy escort you back to your cell. He'll come get you when we hear the D.A.'s decision."

* * *

Almost an hour later, Nick and Moore walked back into the interrogation room.

"Got the confession ready to sign, Conner?" Nick asked.

Conner closed his laptop and handed a copy each to Nick and Moore. Both men focused their attention on the document. There was no room for error.

The deputy opened the door and Conner gave him the go-ahead to bring Tony back. Once again, seated as before, Nick broke the silence. "Your lawyer can relay the details of what we discussed with the District Attorney."

Moore turned to Tony and began, "He's willing to meet us halfway. He wants a confession and the names of the cartel. This way it saves the state the cost of a trial. He'll recommend to the judge the sentence be lowered to second degree murder. You could be looking at fifteen to twenty with possible parole."

Tony rubbed his chin several times as he thought the situation through. Several moments of silence seemed like an eternity, but in the end, he turned to Conner and said, "Where do I sign?"

"Before you do," suggested Nick, "let your lawyer read it to you. We want you to fully comprehend what you've confessed to."

As the words sunk in, tears dribbled down the beaten man's face and Nick handed him the box of tissues. His hand shook as he took the pen and signed his name.

Conner glanced at Nick as they watched the deputy escort Tony back to his cell. "You satisfied with the outcome?"

Nick reached out and picked up the coffee cup that now contained Tony Colbert's DNA. It's always a relief when they sign a confession, but it's this little baby that ultimately seals their fate. I'm on my way to the lab. Yeah, we did our job today. Lights out!"

Chapter Twenty - Six

After the intense investigation into the Mathison case and the apprehension attributed to Hamilton's tip, a week of routine activity almost seemed like a vacation. One evening after work, Nick drove out to the beach, parked his car and walked out to sit on the cushion of white sand. He watched as the waves tumbled over each other and finally sloshed ashore.

His thoughts meandered here and there as his gaze settled on the water that appeared to melt into the horizon. He realized there was life not only on this side of the breakers, but that things happened beyond them that often would never be known. *If Mike Perkins hadn't decided to make one more shrimp run*, he thought, *Craig Mathison's body might never have been found.* Nick sat there until the emerging darkness swallowed up the tangerine sun, leaving room for the shimmering sparkle of a full moon before Nick called it a day and drove home.

* * *

Honored to be best man at Heather and Conner's beach-side wedding, Nick's hard-core persona dissolved like melting snowflakes as he stood by Conner's side on the virgin, white sand and watched Heather as she strolled down the carpeted boardwalk in a gown of chiffon and lace. A light late-afternoon breeze flirted with strands of her wheat-streaked hair that brushed against pink, tinted cheeks.

Once Heather stopped at Conner's side, Nick stepped back and looked at his partner. Unspoken thoughts brought a wash of emotion. *I pray you don't let the intensity of our job suck the life out of your marriage and you turn to alcohol as I did. Believe me, friend, it's a lonely life without the love of the right woman.*

The words of the pastor brought Nick out of his reverie. "And may we have the ring, please?"

Nick's right hand dove into his jacket pocket, extracted a sparkling diamond solitaire. He handed it to Conner with a sigh of relief. Earlier in the day, it seemed that Penny had hounded him every hour. "Dad, you put Heather's wedding ring in your jacket pocket, didn't you? Check to be sure."

The inspirational ceremony, though not lengthy, united the couple. After a round of congratulations and hugs, the celebration began. Nick searched the crowd and found Maureen talking to Penny. *Great*, he thought, *they seem to be hitting it off fine. And that's a good thing.* He walked up to his date and lightly touched her elbow.

Penny rushed in with her tease, "Dad, I didn't take a breath until I saw you hand over the ring."

Maureen, looked stunning with her natural curls pinned behind delicate ears, winked at Nick as she came to his defense. "When the heat is on, I believe you can count on your dad."

"I second that," Penny agreed and kissed her father's cheek. "Now, let's go find some food. I'm starving, and the buffet looks fabulous!"

The usual toasts and speeches to the bride and groom went smoothly, and as the sun sank deeper into the Gulf, the jovial occasion became louder and louder. An open bar did not help temper the festive mood of the guests. Mindful of their AA allegiance, Nick and Maureen wandered off onto the hotel patio. They chatted easily. The months of sharing each other's thoughts and lives at AA meetings had formed a bond.

Maureen seemed mesmerized by the beauty of the shimmering moon beams on the gentle rolling waves. In fact, for a time, she was speechless. Nick sensed the timing was right to ask her to take a walk on the beach with him.

"You know, there's a local folk lore that says if you walk on the beach in the moonlight and leave your footprints in the Santa Rosa Island sand, you'll never leave Florida."

Maureen caught the twinkle in her date's eyes. "You just made every bit of that up, didn't you? But..." She slipped out of her sandals as she reached for Nick's hand. "Guess what? I'm willing to see if it's true."

Nick could have sworn his heart skipped a beat!

About the Author

Sylvia Melvin lives in Milton, Florida. She is an Elementary Intervention teacher.

Her Canadian heritage is often reflected in her writing. She enjoys writing short stories and novels.

As one of the founding members of the Panhandle Writer's Group, she is motivated by her fellow writers and the skills she has learned.

Sylvia is married to an American and has lived in Florida since 1993.

Made in the USA
Columbia, SC
11 March 2018